MISSING

MISSING

Michelle Herman

Ohio State University Press
Columbus

F
H

Library of Congress Cataloging-in-Publication Data

Herman, Michelle.
  Missing / Michelle Herman.
      p.   cm.
  ISBN 0-8142-0503-8 (alk. paper)
  I. Title.
PS3558.E6825M57   1990   89-38340
813'.54 – dc20   CIP

The paper in this book meets the guidelines for permanence and
durability of the Committee on Production Guidelines for Book
Longevity of the Council on Library Resources.

Printed in the U.S.A.

9 8 7 6 5 4 3 2 1

For my grandmother,
Yetta Weingrovitz Weiss,
and for my parents

eyn harts filt dos andere

For support during the writing of this book,
grateful acknowledgment is made
to the National Endowment for the Arts
and to James Michener
and the Copernicus Society of America

No one knows the real truth.

CHEKHOV
The Duel

1

When she discovered that the beads, which she had been saving for so many years, were missing, Rivke at first could not do anything at all. She stood by the bureau, staring down at the little white box in the palm of her hand. "How could it be?" she murmured. "How?" Everything else was where it belonged: the silverplated oval tray with its dusty unused gift bottles of toilet water and cologne; the china bowl full of safety pins and buttons, and the matching saucer that held barrettes and bangles and glass pendants; her carved ivory jewelbox, empty for years, in which she had kept her few pieces of good jewelry before their removal, at the insistence of her children, to a safe deposit box in the bank, four blocks away on Coney Island Avenue; the pink and glitter-speckled brush and comb set, a long-ago gift from the children that must have been meant for show only, the brush's bristles so short and soft they wouldn't have tickled a doll's hair; and the pair of gilt-framed photographs—the first the wedding portrait in which she and Sol looked like two solemn children, the second a picture of them taken a dozen years later, this time flanked by two serious-looking children of their own, and with her pregnant again, and wearing the black dress.

She glanced quickly over everything once more. It had been her habit for decades to begin each day by reassuring herself that all was as it should be. That something would *not* be where she had last laid eyes on it had, however, never occurred to her. Nothing had ever turned up missing before. Of course, she did not ordinarily lift the cover of the cardboard box that had held the beads; so she had no way of knowing how long its contents had been gone. She wished now that she had not checked under the box's lid today—and immediately she was ashamed of herself for this thought. Would not knowing make what was true be untrue? Anyway, she told herself, a more interesting consideration was this: What had caused her to peek into the box today?

Ah, well—she shrugged, and this thought too she dismissed. Interesting maybe, but still a foolish question, one which could not be answered securely. By now she knew that the *why* of such a question—a guess, after all (intuition? impulse? inspiration?)—would be of no help to her; at her age she had no use for guesses that amounted to nothing. In any case the beads were gone. Finished.

She was not surprised to find that she did not feel alarmed. Old age, she had long since learned, stole such instincts— alarm, outrage, pure grief—and left in their place only a single muddled first response to anything unexpected: part bewilderment, part fear. The ringing phone, the realization that she had once again misplaced her keys, a catastrophe announced on the six o'clock news—any surprise at all triggered this moment of confused anxiety. It was only after this had passed that she was able to experience the ordinary reaction, whatever it was that she might have felt in her youth.

Or even—she thought with a sigh—long after her youth had passed. This paralysis of feelings was, after all, by her measure a recent development: perhaps ten years or twelve had passed since it had set in; yet she had not been young now for several decades. She often had to remind herself of this. "Old, old, old," she would mutter as she made her way from room to room. "Not only old. Elderly. Ancient. A ruin." But as she shuffled through the foyer, a glance in the mirror there would challenge her, plainly submitting its evidence to the contrary; for as she approached her ninetieth birthday she was still a woman of considerable beauty. This was something of which

2

she could hardly be unaware. She passed daily before the circle of mirror that had hung in the foyer just outside the bathroom for more than sixty years, confirming each day that her
looks were holding yet. Her face was still—miraculously—free
of all but the most delicate wrinkles; her skin was quite pink,
unspotted and without even the slightest gray cast, that shadowed look she had begun years ago to recognize on the faces
of her old neighbors. She was lucky, she knew it. She had a
fine head of hair, white curls as weightless and pleasant to
touch as a handful of goosedown, and her eyes were clear still,
a good blue, holding their light behind the stylishly framed
bifocals her daughter had selected for her.

Her looks had in fact been softened to their advantage by
age. Young, she had been a soldier of a woman: stocky and
square-shouldered, unsmiling in repose, her dark thick hair
contained by a tightly wound duet of braids. Now a gentler
aspect had emerged that she could see herself was becoming.
Confronting the mirror, she would puff out her cheeks, cup
her curls in her hands, and shake her head. "Just look at yourself,
Rivke," she would murmur. "Just look at you."

Her figure, too, was remarkably good—womanly, even ro-
bust. Only months before his death, her husband, himself
some years over ninety—even Rivke did not know his exact
age, for she had never asked and he had never volunteered
it—had confided in their daughter that coming upon Rivke
in the bath he found the sight of her "very exciting. Still!" he
had told Myra. "No less than ever. But you know"—and Rivke
could just imagine his wink and his upturned hand as he lowered his voice, confessing—"at an age like this, there's plenty
you can't any longer manage." This admission apparently had
embarrassed Myra, who had repeated it to her own daughter,
Rachel. Rachel, however, was Rivke's confidante; thus the remark was passed along, and Rivke, when she heard it, chuckled. "Oh, sure," she said. "He wants his fun. But enough fun
he's had already. The time for that is finished." "Is that so?"

3

Rachel said. "If you want *my* opinion, it could be that Papa might actually manage perfectly well, if you'd just give him the chance to try." Rivke laughed again. Rachel was her favorite; she could get away with murder.

Rachel, in truth, was not merely her favorite, she was the only one of her grandchildren who was of importance to her. This of course was not something one could talk about. Rivke kept it to herself; this was necessary in order to spare the feelings of her children, who assumed she felt a strong attachment to *their* children. But—first of all—there were too many. How could she be deeply attached to every one of them? Particularly when she so rarely saw them? And it was not as if she disliked them—that would be unnatural, to dislike one's own grandchildren. It was only that of her many grandchildren (and there were a number of great-grandchildren too, and even one great-great-grandchild; this was an extraordinary fact that startled her anew each time she thought of it), Rachel alone was *real* to her. Occasionally she felt troubled by this—but it was not her fault; this was what she explained to herself. Was it her fault that she did not know the other children as she knew Rachel, the daughter of her only daughter? The others were like ghosts to her, all these boys and girls (no, men and women now—always she had to remind herself of this) who resembled her children but were not *her* children, who resembled, too, her own mother, her husband's brothers, half-forgotten cousins left long ago in Poland. The *idea* of grandchildren was fine, it was even satisfying—so many busy young people, not one of whom would exist if not for her impulsive marriage at sixteen—yet the idea did not amount to anything.

And to them, to these children, she knew *she* was an idea, not something real: a grandmother only, a woman who was old and had always been so. One would think she had been born old. But to Rachel? With Rachel it was another matter entirely. As a child of four or five Rachel had ventured once

4

that she wished she could have known her grandmother as
a little girl. This was a remark Rivke had never forgotten, she
had been so much moved by it. And thus it was by the child
that her own wistfulness had been stirred—that which for
years she had been guarding against. She even caught herself
wondering what it *would* have been to have known Rachel at
her own age, the two of them children together, young girls,
young women. Oh, but what a thought! She had to laugh at
herself. She had been close to sixty when Rachel was born.
Already old. And she had managed for sixty years not to look
back—nearly always she had managed; when she did not suc-
ceed, when just for a moment she could not resist taking a
look backwards, she took her look without sentiment. For
what, anyway, should she feel sentimental? For the years of
hard work? What was there in those years worth clucking and
wringing one's hands over? Only, perhaps, what had *not* been,
what she had not done—and this was something she did not
care to think about; there was no sense in it.

So she did not look back. But the memories were there—
locked up, but undamaged. Sixty years had passed, and then
came the child Rachel—bless her, this child—and the child
would not allow the years to rest. *She* acted as if she had
missed something, waiting to be born. *What happened before?*
she wanted to know. *And what happened next? Next? And after
that?* As a small child she begged Rivke to talk about the old
country, about her own mother and father, about coming to
America, about the time when she had lived on Essex Street,
the Lower East Side, with her sister Leah, during the months
before she married Sol and the two of them scurried off to
Brooklyn like thieves. And now she was a grown woman, and
she had not given up: *still* she was after Rivke for informa-
tion—still she wanted to know everything. To see her rake
through old photographs—this was something to see! She
would look and look, making little piles of them, little slipping
and sliding mountains, and then she would select one and

study it as if she thought she might etch the image onto her heart. Ten minutes, fifteen, she would sit examining a single photograph. Looking for what? Rivke wondered as she watched her. *For clues*, she thought. For clues to something—Rivke didn't know what.

Rachel would hold up the picture for her to see; she would stab at the faces of her relations with one pointed finger: "Who is this, Grandma? And this, next to him? Why is this one so sad?" She demanded facts—personalities, occupations, years married, birthplaces, adventures, causes of death—to match the faces. Many of these people had died before her birth. Some, who as far as Rivke knew were still alive, she knew nothing else about. There was a branch of her family, springing from her youngest sister, Sheine, that was in Argentina; for fifty years Rivke had been receiving photographs of unknown nieces and nephews, strangers in wedding dresses, mysterious dark-eyed babies. What could Rivke tell her granddaughter about such people? But there were also pictures in which Rachel was able to recognize a face from her childhood. "My God, that's Tante Etke, isn't it?" she would say; she was amazed herself that she could recognize her old aunt. Under Rivke's nose she waved the picture: Sol's eldest sister, here a girl of sixteen standing stiffly before a painted backdrop, ribboned hat in hand, innocent of what would become the facts of her life—that she would marry a shoemaker, bear five sons and outlive all of them, sons and husband both; that she would lose her speech to the first of two strokes that came to her a decade apart; that she would be great-aunt to the child Rachel, who twenty-five years after the second stroke had taken her would ask, "What was she like? How close was she to Papa? Were you fond of her?"

"Ah, Rucheleh, I never knew her so well myself," Rivke told her.

"But what did you *think* of her? Did you like her? Were you friends? Did Papa love her very much?"

6

"I think she was a good woman," Rivke said. "She was always kind to me, she had a good nature. Friends?" She had to smile at her granddaughter. "Friends we weren't. Who had time to sit talking? Also you have to remember she was much older than me, she was much older than Papa too. Eleven years, twelve years older, something like that. She took care of him from the time when he was a baby. His mama died before he was a year old—this I'm sure you remember. So Etke was like a mother to him more than a sister. Naturally he loved her. But more than this I can't tell you. We didn't talk so much about these things then."

"Still, he must have been very attached to her. I remember him making a big fuss over her."

"She was sick," Rivke said. "For a long time, for years, she was sick. From before you were born. Sure he made a fuss, he worried about her. He was always afraid for her." She shook her head. "You were such a small kid when Etke died—five years old, six years old. How is it that you remember any of this?"

"But I hardly can at all. That's the point. That's why I want *you* to try to remember."

So Rivke would try—how could she say no? She looked over the photographs Rachel handed her; she searched in her memory for details. Often, however, to remember was impossible. So many of these photographs were of people to whom she had paid little attention; others she had on purpose forgotten. A few of them upset her so much—photographs of her sister Essie's husband, or of Sol's brother Moishe, who had said such terrible things about her, or of certain of her sons' old girlfriends—she could not speak of them at all. Sometimes she was unable to prevent herself from snatching a photograph out of Rachel's hand; she would fold it again and again until it was a tiny useless square which she tucked into her apron pocket to be thrown down the incinerator chute later.

"Removing the villains?" Rachel would say.

"Don't raise up your eyebrows to me," Rivke would tell her.

"There are some people it's better to forget. This you'll learn later."

From time to time they would come to a picture of a group of people, and someone Rivke could not bear to remember would appear there. She kept manicure scissors handy for this purpose, and she would carefully cut away the small oval that contained the offending face. This made Rachel groan. "*Grandma*, this is impossible. How can you do that?"

"How?" Rivke snorted. "How! Essie's husband, that murderous bastard—you should pardon me—why should I care to look at his face? When I'm dead there will be no one left who can remember him. That's how it should be. Better that he should be taken out of everybody's mind forever."

"But it won't happen anyway," Rachel said. "I'll remember. I've heard all those terrible stories about him."

"Better you should forget too," Rivke told her.

"Then what's the *point?*" Rachel said. "You think you can change what was by ignoring it? You want to rewrite your own history? What are you, a Communist country?"

Rivke shrugged politely. The *argument* was what was pointless, as far as she was concerned. If the history of her family needed to be rewritten just a little—well, it was *her* history, they were *her* photographs. Though how it had happened that she had come into the possession of so many photographs was a mystery to her. She had hundreds, thousands of them: boxes and boxes full. If pictures were bricks, she liked to tell Rachel, she could build a little house for herself, she wouldn't have to live anymore in this apartment she had grown to hate. She had pictures enough for ten families, for twenty; she had pictures of everyone: her children at each stage of their lives, and their children and their children's children; her brothers and sisters, and her husband's brothers and sisters, and her *and* her husband's brothers' and sisters' children, grandchildren, great-grandchildren. And then there were all the unidentifiable ones, the snapshots that had been sent to her by people who did not even bother to write the name of the newborn infant or *bar mitzve* boy on the back. When one of these arrived, Rivke would glance at it and set it down, along with the note that came with it, on the kitchen table, where greeting cards and letters and advertisements accumulated; eventually, when she decided to straighten up the kitchen, the cards and the notes and the junk mail would be thrown away, and the picture would be dropped into one of the boxes. In a year, or even in a month or two, she would not be able to determine which branch of the family was responsible for this one.

So many pictures! Rivke had no idea who had taken most of them, not even the ones of herself and the children when the children were young. There had always been someone with a camera, ready to shoot at the drop of a hat. And she herself, owner of all these pictures, had never owned a camera. "Maybe I'm meant to make up for that," Rachel would say, for she had several; she was a photographer—this was the career she had chosen. A strange career, Rivke thought, more like play than work. And lately, as a sort of hobby ("a project" was what she called it), Rachel had decided to undertake the task of organizing Rivke's photographs. Rivke had told her not to bother; there were too many, they spanned too many years, and too many obscure family paths would have to be traced and would come to nothing; everywhere there were dead ends. Rachel, however, insisted. She wanted, at least, to separate out the ancient ones from the more recent and the very recent, she said. And yet, each time she visited, after hours spent pawing through a great heap of them, she would temporarily abandon her plan and instead only stuff a fresh batch of photographs into her satchel to take home. Rivke would laugh at her. "Soon you'll have as many as I do, and then you'll be sorry. Boxes upon boxes you'll have."

But Rachel did not fill boxes with the photographs she brought back to her apartment in New York ("Manhattan," she corrected Rivke, again and again. "Call it Manhattan; it's *all* New York"). She pasted them into albums, with notations below them of the details she had extracted from Rivke. A dozen or so of her favorites Rachel had framed and hung on her walls; occasionally she would add another. And she had photographed the walls and brought these photographs to Rivke. It was astonishing to see—all those pictures of herself! But first she had had to get over the shock of what she saw of the apartment itself—the bathtub in the kitchen, just as it had been in her sister Leah's place on Essex Street seventy-five years ago, and all the rooms so small and square, and crammed full of furniture. And such clutter! And yet it wasn't an unpleasant clutter, she concluded after looking for a long time at the photographs. Everything was in a jumble—there was no system to it that she could see—but it was a happy mess, it was lively, and this appealed to her. Nice things, little boxes and scarves and vases full of dried flowers, were mixed in with the stacks of books and the heaps of clothes, and the effect of everything together was cozy; one might even say pretty. Here and there were shawls and strips of lace for decoration; rugs were set atop rugs; round pillows and hanging beads, seashells and candlesticks were scattered about everywhere. Rivke was fascinated by the look of the rooms. She had the feeling that everything about them had been exactly as it was forever—a strange feeling, but a good one. "Timelessness?" Rachel asked her when she tried to explain. "Is that the feeling you mean?"—But it was not time*less*ness she felt—not an absence. It was time's great, silent presence: time solid and holding still; or, at the very least—*holding still* was of course saying too much; and she knew better, she did not say it aloud—time keeping its steady eye on things. Time watching, keeping its own counsel, Rivke thought. Time behaving itself.

In the photographs of her that Rachel had chosen to hang, decades clashed peacefully. Over the mantelpiece she was fourteen, newly arrived in this country; over the couch she was thirty, caught surprised in her then-still-new kitchen. In the

bedroom she was both fifty, posing frowning on the boardwalk, and sixteen, in a hand-tinted, elaborately framed copy
of her wedding portrait; in the kitchen she was approaching
forty, her head bowed as she stood on Brighton Beach Avenue, a baby carriage at her side. Other pictures from her collection were here too—one of Sol alone, young and round-
cheeked and beautifully dressed, holding tight to a thick book
that must have been a prop supplied by the photographer;
one—very stern—of Rivke's parents, whom Rachel had never
known (in the case of her father, Rivke had had to explain,
the sternness was an accident of the camera, untrue to his
character; her mother, however, appeared here as she had appeared to Rivke every day of her life); and, side by side, a
studio portrait of Myra as a teenager, smiling brilliantly, and
one of her as a very young child suspended in Rivke and Sol's
arms. These pictures of Myra Rachel had hung over her desk—a
square squeezed between couch and bookcase in a corner of
her living room—and, just above them, in an oval frame of
carved wood, she had centered a photograph of herself, posed
ladylike at three in lace-trimmed dark velvet, ankles and palms
crossed, on the edge of Rivke's bed.

Along with all the old photographs hung a number of
Rachel's own: those oddly angled and shadowed views of children at play that were almost disturbing, that would *be* disturbing, Rivke thought, if one did not know that the activity
in them—the pushing and pulling around swings and slides;
the deep-digging in black-streaked sand; the upside-down sprawl
from a metal jungle of bars, a head dangling only inches from
cement ground—was meant to be joyous; as well as the few still
lifes of plants, their broad, veiny leaves making black shadows
like stains behind them, and several of Rachel's strange, gloomy
portraits, including one of Rivke that Rivke did not like at all.
Of the many photographs of her that Rachel had taken, there
were quite a few that pleased Rivke—those for which Rachel
had allowed her to dress up and pose properly, brush her hair

and remove her glasses—but these were the ones her grand-daughter liked least. In the one Rachel had selected to hang in her living room, Rivke looked, she thought, uncharacteristically like her own mother: harsh and unyielding—even threatening; she wielded a long spoon like a weapon. The kitchen loomed cavelike around her where she stood glowering by the stove—Rachel had taken her by surprise as she was reheating a pot of soup—her hair escaping untidily from a crooked ponytail, a wrinkled apron around her waist, her brows knit as if she were furious.

"The great matriarch," Rachel had teased her when she'd first presented Rivke with a print. "You're a little terrifying, you know that?" But it did not seem to Rivke that there was anything funny about this picture. "This is not what I look like," she said. "This is *nothing* like what I look like." When Rachel brought over the most recent photographs of her apartment and pointed out that she had hung the portrait directly opposite the door, so that this image of Rivke was the first sight encountered upon entering the apartment, Rivke was distressed. "You couldn't have picked a nicer one?" she asked her. "A nicer one? This is my favorite picture of you," Rachel said. "Except, of course, for *that* one"—and she waved a hand in the direction of Rivke's bedroom. The one she meant, Rivke knew, was the formal portrait in which she stood with Sol and the two oldest boys. Very often they had talked about this picture. Rachel said she liked it because it told a story, and this Rivke appreciated and approved of—she liked it for this reason too, and not *just* because it told a story, but because it was a story that could not be easily explained in words or be understood by a stranger who was taking a casual look. In this picture, which had been made just after they had moved into the apartment in Brighton Beach, there was a glimpse of the years to come. Rivke, not yet thirty—younger then than Rachel!—had already had two children and two miscarriages; another child was to come within months. And here, in her face, she thought, was something that would appear in every picture of her forever after—this was something that had never shown in her before. *This* was the story the photograph held: it told of how she had changed, how something inside her had by then turned hard, had tightened and set in her and had changed her forever. Not only her—they had both changed by this time, both she and Sol. Look at him in this picture, look how vague and distracted he was! This was new, this had not been his way before—had it? Had he not changed as much as she? This faraway look—this was how it was to be for the rest of his life. And she, with her lips drawn tightly together, her head held so straight and her chin pulled up, she looked bound and determined—but for what? For *what* was she so prepared? There had been a time when she had stood staring trying to identify precisely what it was this picture could tell her about herself; but she had given this up, long ago she had given this up, and now, each morning, she only glanced at the picture as she glanced at everything else. Certainly she did not think about it; she did not really look at it. Today, however—it could not be helped—her eyes were drawn back to it, and there her gaze remained. How grim she looked! How *severe*. And yet, she thought, not unattractive—not in that dress. It had been impossible to look unattractive in that dress.

Oh, that dress! What a dress it had been! Exquisite—a miracle of a dress, its thick black silk embroidered with an intricate pattern of black crystal beads that so weighted down the dress its thin straps seemed barely able to support its weight. Sol had bought the dress for her when they discovered that she was pregnant for the first time, a year after they were married. It was an extravagance, they could not afford it, and this had been one of the very few times he had prevailed in this way, spending money when she had forbidden him to do so. The dress was meant to be worn while she was pregnant—he had bought it several sizes too large—and she had worn it once or perhaps twice before miscarrying; afterwards she had put it away. "I'm sorry," she told him, "for the waste of money. But I can't look at it."

When she became pregnant again she thought of the dress but finally left it where it was; it seemed foolish to tempt fate. Then Amos was born, and, four years later, pregnant with La-zar, she again briefly considered wearing the dress and again decided against it. When she became pregnant for the fourth time the dress did not even enter her mind; when she miscar-ried this time she hardened against future disappointments. It was during her next pregnancy that she unwrapped the dress, posing in it for the family portrait Sol insisted they have made—another extravagance, but one over which she hadn't the energy to argue.

The dress had long ago disintegrated—she had worn it to death; for once she began wearing it, she wore it and wore it, wore it to weddings and *bar mitzves* and even funerals, wore it during pregnancies and between pregnancies (at first it was far too big to wear when she wasn't pregnant, but as the years and pregnancies added up, her shape changed so that it fit better when she was not pregnant than when she was, and did not fit at all during the final months of her last preg-nancy)—but she had saved the crystal beads, every one that she was able to salvage as they fell from the silk, and for years now she had been promising herself that she would make a long necklace of these beads as a gift for Rachel, a necklace that Rachel could wrap and wrap around her neck so that it fell across her chest in sparkling loops; she could *see* it, she could imagine it glittering just as the dress had glittered.

This intention—and also the beads themselves—Rivke had for a long time kept secret, but six or eight months ago she had taken out the cardboard box which she had been hiding in a bureau drawer and she had shown the beads to Rachel.

"Yes, of course," Rachel said when Rivke told her that they were from an old dress. "The beautiful black dress in the picture."

Rivke had resolved then to get to work on the necklace

immediately. Yet somehow she had put it off; she knew what a difficult job it would be, and she was afraid to find out just how difficult. Her eyes became easily strained, and her fingers were not so agile as they had once been. Not so agile? Her fingers were almost useless—they felt thick and clumsy, they would not grasp things as they were meant to. So she had put it off, hoping to get stronger though she knew this was impossible. And now it was plain that she had put it off too long.

How can it be? she asked herself. How could the beads be missing? How could they have disappeared, just like that, when she had been keeping them for so long?

She would have to tell Rachel, she thought. And it was only now—now, as she imagined telling her granddaughter, the only person living to whom she could open her heart even a crack—that she began to feel alarmed. The alarm came in a rush, and was followed instantly by a feeling of outrage that rose in her with such force she gasped and rocked backwards on her heels. For a moment she stood panting, trying only to steady her breathing. Then her fist came down hard on the bureau—too hard, a stupid thing to do. The pain that filled her fist felt like fury itself.

Impossible! Unfair!

She moved away from the bureau, backing up to the bed, where she lowered herself slowly until she was sitting. Delayed her feelings might be, she thought bitterly, but when they came, they came with all the force that was required. This was something else she had discovered about old age. It took nothing away utterly—what it took from one was the power to experience things quickly, fully. It left one with one's old own self— with enough of what was necessary to continue—but with every reaction, every thought and every motion, slowed and dimmed and crippled. It seemed to her that this might be worse than complete loss.

The box was still in her hand—she was surprised to find it there. Her other hand, the one she'd hurt, she placed gently in her lap like something separate from her that was in pain. After a little while she took the hand up again, and shook it lightly; she used it to turn the box over, letting fall into her lap the few remaining threadbare strands of black silk she had kept in with the beads. She ran her index finger over the bed of cotton inside the box and then around the edges of the box itself. Pointless gestures. Not a single bead remained – she had seen that from the beginning, from the instant she had removed the lid.

She set the box down in her lap. Gone. The beads were gone, the box was empty, and all that was left were the few pathetic scraps of the silk that had once been the dress upon which the beads had hung. How long *had* she been saving them? A long, long time – too long to count. *Gone.* She began now to tremble. *Gone* – gone! But *gone* was too nice a word. *Taken. Stolen.*

Someone had taken them, of that she was certain. At her age, it was necessary to be certain at all times. To doubt anything for more than a few seconds made it become true, or at least made it seem so nearly true as to be impossible to dispute. She knew that when she told Myra the beads were gone, she would be accused at once of mislaying them; it was essential that she be prepared to dismiss this charge without the instant of hesitation that would encourage Myra to insist that she was right.

Halfheartedly, then – less than halfheartedly: she had no heart for this at all, nor had she the strength – she hoisted herself off the bed and began to move about the room, searching. She turned over the pillows on the unused bed (she never slept in the bed anymore, not since Sol was gone; she slept, or tried and failed to sleep, on the couch in the living room) and opened all the drawers in the bureau and the two nightstands, poking under the clothes stacked neatly within. She ran her hands over surfaces she was not tall enough to see – the top of the chifforobe, the uppermost shelf of the closet.

For a minute she sat down again and made a plan for what she knew would be a futile search of the rest of the apartment. Then she went from room to room, opening and closing closet doors and cabinet shutters, pushing things, peeking under things, sighing all the while. Nothing. So—gone is gone, she thought grimly as she completed the search.

And now what? she wondered. She thought about calling Rachel. To call Myra was out of the question—this was something she never did. Anyway, if she waited she would hear from Myra soon enough; she called every morning. But Rachel? No, she decided against that too. Rachel she did call sometimes, but it was always an ordeal: it took such a great effort to locate the phone number and then it was difficult for her to dial—the tiny printed numbers on the telephone wobbled before her eyes—and finally there was the possibility of reaching, instead of her granddaughter, the answering machine Rachel used when she was at her part-time job or in the darkroom. To talk to a machine made Rivke feel foolish; she could not stand to say "This is your grandmother" to the machine. So she could wait for Rachel's call also. She was likely to call in the evening; she did this almost without fail. So it was settled: for now there was nothing to do but wait. And was there something new about that? "When you're old," she often said to Rachel, "all you do is wait."

And think, she added to herself as she headed for the kitchen. Waiting and thinking—the only two activities for which she was now suited.

In the kitchen she turned on the black-and-white TV and filled the kettle with water and set it to boil. This was her morning routine and she felt uneasy about its having been disrupted. Now, with the TV murmuring companionably, she began to feel a little better, and she eased herself into her customary chair, beside the radiator pipe, and closed her eyes. It didn't take much to tire her out, and this business had exhausted her.

17

Who would do such a thing? she thought. Who would steal from her? She squeezed her eyes shut to help her concentrate as she began to consider the possibilities. Myra and Rachel both, it went without saying, were above suspicion. But she had talked about the beads to entirely too many people, she saw now. Once she had spoken of them to Rachel, she had become so excited by the prospect of making a necklace she had spoken of her plan to her sons. They, of course, were not to be suspected either. But their wives, their children and their grandchildren, that was something else altogether. Sons told wives, wives told children, and so on. This could not be helped.

Who? She tried to recall when she had last seen the beads. She had, in the months since she had shown them to Rachel, felt moved to open the box a number of times, just for the pleasure of looking at the beads and touching them—how they brought things back to her! The feel of that dress, those years! But she could not remember the last time she had done this. A few weeks, a few months ago?

To be safe, she thought, assume months. And who had been in her apartment in the last few months? Well, who ever came to see her, after all? Not many people: her daughter, her sons, her sons' wives. In the last few weeks the only wife to visit had been May; she and Sammy had spent a Sunday with her. As far as Rivke could recall, she had not left the living room, not even to go to the bathroom. This was how it always was with May. She had sat stiffly on the couch and had hardly said a word. *Registering a protest,* Rivke had thought, unamused but not concerned either, as she sat listening to Sammy talk and watching his wife's lips twitch and her eyes flick from side to side in her mask of a face. No, not May. If she were going to steal something, it would be *something.* Not a boxful of beads that were worth more in memories, in history, than in money. She was a businesswoman, that one. A thing like this would be beneath her notice. All right, who then? Rivke drew her hands to her face and pressed her fingers to her eyelids. *Think.*

18

Frances, Amos's wife, had been here once or twice in the last few months, but she could be easily dismissed. She was barely able to walk now—she was more unsteady on her feet than Rivke was—and throughout her visits she had lain on the couch, whining for her husband's attention.

Some wives, Rivke thought, and her lip curled involuntarily. Some messes my children have gotten themselves into.

Over the television's soft chatter (a discussion show, Rivke's favorite kind) she could hear the gurgle of water boiling, and holding on to the table she pulled herself up and made her way to the stove. She proceeded to fill a mug—a nice one, decorated with tiny pink and yellow flowers, a gift from Rachel—with hot water and a squeeze of lemon. Perhaps Rachel would have an idea about who had stolen the beads. But at this thought, with which she had meant to console herself, she was reminded once again that she had not yet told Rachel about the theft, and again she felt herself becoming agitated. She was so disturbed that as she returned to the table her hand shook and hot water splashed from the mug. With her attention focused on this, she did not at first realize that the phone had begun to ring; then, when she did, she remained motionless, half-full mug in hand, her heart hammering, for six or seven rings—the six or seven that she heard—until finally her fear receded and she was able to move toward the phone on the wall beside the refrigerator.

"Yes? Who is it?"

"Mama, hi, it's me."

Myra. Good. Her relief felt almost like happiness. "Good morning, *tokhter*. How do you feel?"

"All right. How do *you* feel?"

"How should I feel?" Rivke laughed. "How do you think I feel?"

"You took a long time to get to the phone."

"I always take a long time. You move slower when you're old, you'll see." Then, before Myra had a chance to say anything, she went on quickly: "Myraleh, you know those beads I've been saving?"

"Which beads, Mama?" Rivke could hear a very small— almost but not quite contained—sigh, and she prickled with irritation: the least Myra could do was hide her impatience.

"From my dress, the black dress."

"Which black dress?"

"Which black dress," Rivke murmured.

Myra was silent.

"My black dress. I'm wearing it in the picture on the bureau—you know the picture. With the beads on it. The dress with the beads on it, the beads I've been saving to make a necklace for Rachel."

"Oh, yes, Ma, I remember now." There was no conviction in her voice, however.

"The black crystal beads I've been saving."

"*Yes*, Mama. I told you, I remember."

"Myraleh, they're gone. Someone took them."

"What do you mean?"

"Someone took them and left me the empty box. The least they could have done was to take the box too. Do I need an empty box to look at?"

"What do you mean someone took them? Who could have taken them?"

"Who is right."

"But who would do that? Nobody would do that. Where did you see them last? You must have misplaced them."

"No." Rivke spoke firmly but did not raise her voice. "Someone took them. Don't talk nonsense. Now I ask you: Who comes in here? Strangers don't come in here."

"Mama, really. I don't understand this. What do you mean someone took them? Who do you think could have taken them?"

"I can't say. You think about it, see who you think. Who comes in here?"

"This is silly, Ma."

"So it's silly. Tell me: Who comes?"

"I do. And Rachel. You think we took your beads?"

"Don't talk so foolishly. Naturally I don't think you took them. Think, darling, who else comes?"

"Amos and Frances. Lazar and Ruby and Sammy. May. Naomi."

"Naomi! Naomi hasn't been here for months. Lazar himself hasn't been here for months. Ruby's wife, that witch, you know—"

"Yes, Ma, I know she doesn't come over."

"Won't set foot in my house. Reuben comes alone—if he comes. And when was the last time *he* was here? I don't think I would recognize him if I saw him."

"All right, Mama, that lets out Naomi and Sally. Does that mean you think that Frances or May took your beads? What were those beads made of, anyhow?"

"No, I don't think Frances or May took them. If they were pearls, diamonds, maybe . . . but not these beads."

"Well, the only other person I can think of who comes into your house is Debbie, and you know she—"

Ah, Debbie! "I forgot altogether about her," Rivke murmured.

"Oh, now, Mama, I didn't mean to put any ideas into your head. Debbie wouldn't take your beads, you know that."

Debbie! Rivke shook her head. First of all, was that a name for a grown woman? And a grandmother yet! This was hard to believe—Amos's daughter a grandmother. But her daughter, Amy, had just had a baby, Rivke's first great-great-grandchild. Amy herself was only eighteen. Still, there it was: Debbie had her first grandchild; she was a grandmother at forty. And she had always been strange, even as a small child. This was her mother's fault; Frances had made her strange.

"She stayed over a couple of weeks ago," Rivke said.

"I remember."

"She said to me: 'Grandma, you could use the company.'"

"Mama, don't get started on Debbie. I'm sure you just misplaced them, and they'll turn up, like everything always does."

Rivke bristled. "What 'everything'? Plenty of things have been missing and have stayed missing."

"All right, Ma. I didn't mean to upset you."

"You didn't upset me. What's to upset me?" Better to change the subject, Rivke thought. "So, how is Harry?"

"Fine."

"His back is feeling better?"

"It was only a little strain, Ma, and that was two weeks ago. He's fine now. He's *been* fine."

"So when do you think I'll see you? I know he likes to keep his wife around—who can blame him?—especially when he's not feeling well."

"Mama, why do you make it sound like he keeps me from coming over there? He encouraged me to go out to Brooklyn, to spend the night even if I want to. I've just been very busy, and very tired. I promise I'll get there this week."

Rivke breathed quietly into the phone. "Good," she said. "That's good. Then we can look together to see what else is missing."

"What else is missing?"

"Things." As she said this it surprised her to realize that it was true. Hadn't she looked just yesterday . . . for what? Ah, for Sol's Workmen's Circle pin, which had been on his dark brown jacket, and wasn't it gone? "A lot of things," she said stiffly. "But this is not to talk about on the phone. Now you're busy, you have a friend to have lunch with today, I bet—am I right?"

"You're right."

"Which friend?"

"Norma. You remember Norma? You met her at—"

"I remember. From the carpets."

"Her husband's in the carpet business, right. You know, Ma, sometimes you surprise me."

"Ha," Rivke said.

"We're going to lunch and then to the Metropolitan Museum."

"In New York? Ah, but you're so tired; you should be resting."

"No, Ma, I don't . . . I need. . . ." She began to stammer. Rivke closed her eyes. Myra had been cured of this habit long ago; after her marriage it had surfaced again. She had cured the child of stammering herself! Why it should have come back, she didn't understand. Every time, it made her angry. Nothing stayed put, she thought. Nothing. She waited while her daughter struggled to regain control. Myra managed now to say, "This *is* restful. Besides, I don't have to drive or anything. Norma's driving into the city. She's picking me up."

"All right, darling, that's good. Have a wonderful time. When I see you, we'll talk."

She hung up quickly, as she always did once it was evident that a conversation was over, and set the mug down on the counter—she had been holding it all this time; she had forgotten about it. She would need more hot water anyway. For now she wanted only to think. She was shaken by what she herself had said—that other things were missing. It was true: many things were gone. But she had been allowing her mental list of these missing items to grow and grow, without noticing how long the list had become. She returned to the table and sank into her seat. This was terrible—a terrible problem, and she had been letting it go on. Why *hadn't* she told anyone? Because until today nothing important had been missing? But it was all important—Sol's pin that he had been so proud of, the silk scarf that Myra had brought her from Paris years ago, the hammer—a hammer!—that she had had since the second year of her marriage, which she had discovered was missing when she'd needed to pry a nail out of the wall and had looked for the first time in years in the tool drawer. It was *all* important.

She reached out to flip the dial on the TV, settled on channel two and another discussion show, a nicely dressed group

23

of young women looking serious, and as she sat back, drum-
ming her fingers on the table, at once the answer came to her.
She had not spoken of this because she had not herself believed it. Nothing had been *missing*; this was not the word she
had used to describe her losses to herself. Losses were losses,
lost. What gets lost also gets found—this stood to reason. "Wait,
you'll find again"—this was what she had said to herself. And
she had been wrong. It was time now to admit this. It was time
to face what was true. Gone was gone and would not be found.
Someone was taking her things. Next matter to face: What
was she to do?

The first task—this much was clear—was to figure out who
was doing this to her. "Who would do that?" Myra had said.
"Nobody would do that." Well, somebody had. The only question was who.

Who was responsible for this?

She remembered Myra's remark about Debbie. It was a good
thing Myra had thought of her; Rivke might have overlooked
this possibility. But how could she have forgotten that Debbie
had spent the night here? All that talk about how this would
be a treat for her grandmother! Well, Rivke had slept better
than usual that night, it was true. She was not so tense as she
was most nights, knowing for once that there was someone
else in the apartment. Still, that did not mean Debbie had not
taken the beads. If she knew about them, and about the
necklace—and she might; Rivke could not remember if she
had said anything to her; it was always hard to remember
what she had said or not said, it became so easily mixed up
with what she had thought, or thought of saying and decided
against saying, or meant to say and forgotten to say—then
there was a chance that she might have taken them. She might
have done this out of spite alone. She was jealous of Rachel,
of Rivke's affection for her, Rivke was certain. Debbie was
the only other one of all of them who bothered with Rivke,
who thought to call or visit sometimes—the only other one

besides Rachel's brother, Mark (but he was another story, Rivke thought; he *used* to call, he used to come: since his marriage, Rivke hardly ever saw him anymore) — and she must be tired of hearing Rachel this, Rachel that. "Well," Rivke said aloud, her eyes on the little TV set, where "The Price Is Right" was just starting up, "if it's a case like this. . . ."

She leaned back, tipping the chair against the radiator pipe. She could simply ask her: "Debbie darling, do you know those beads I've been saving? Have you seen them?" But that was perhaps too obvious.

Obvious! She snapped forward in her chair. It had just occurred to her — the thought rising like smoke from another, smoldering thought abandoned — that she was forgetting someone, a much *more* obvious choice. Had she not just this moment been thinking about Mark, Myra's son, and the change in him since his marriage? And had he not brought his new wife with him on a visit not long ago? Rhonda, her name was. Now here was a real possibility. Mark had been married to her for less than a year, and who knew anything about her?

Rivke tried to remember their visit. She shut her eyes, imagining the girl, Rhonda — skinny, not unpretty — as she poked around the rooms, complimenting Rivke on the same things she had seen on every one of her visits. Each time, she oohed and aahed again. She was not a bad girl, there was nothing wrong with her, but still. . . . Mark was such a beautiful boy — smart, good; he had a heart of gold. And this girl? She was not for him, Rivke felt this strongly. And didn't Rachel feel the same way? What exactly had she said? "We don't have much to say to each other"? They didn't care for each other. So it was certainly possible — likely, even — that the girl was jealous of Rachel. And perhaps Rivke had made the mistake of talking about the beads to her and Mark. And so Rhonda had taken them as — as what? Here Rivke was at a loss. As a prank? To be cruel? Just because she thought they were pretty? Could she be one of those people you saw on television who could not keep themselves from stealing? *Kleptomaniacs*, Rivke thought, gratified that she was able to remember the word.

Had the girl gone into the bedroom, come upon the beads by accident, and decided that she wanted them? Or had Rivke perhaps brought them out to show her, and later had Rhonda crept into the bedroom and emptied them into her purse? No, if she had shown them she would remember, wouldn't she? But she might have spoken of them – of this she couldn't be sure. It was so frustrating not to be able to remember! And she could remember so easily every last detail of her childhood in Poland!

Well, what could be the truth? Maybe it was her own fault. Maybe she had been thoughtless enough to flaunt the beads, and flaunt her plans for them, and the child simply had not been able to help herself.

But that was surely nonsense. No one was forced to steal someone else's things. And what, in any case, was she to do about this? She could not accuse Mark's wife of stealing. This was something her grandson would not tolerate, an accusation like this. It would make him furious – he had a temper like a bomb exploding, a temper like his father's – and he would not forgive her, ever. She knew that he had not forgiven Amos for a remark he'd made, distraught, while Sol lay dying in the hospital. Rivke had heard the explosion then herself and she had rushed, astonished, from Sol's bedside into the corridor, where Mark stood bellowing at his uncle because he had suggested that it would be better if "real family, blood relations only" – not Rhonda, then, and not Mark's father, Harry – should be allowed into the room to sit with Sol. Such yelling and such screaming as she had never heard before, she'd heard from Mark that day.

No, she thought, she would not risk offending him.

So what then was to be done? What *could* be done? She blinked and stretched, and restlessly she looked around. There was not so much to see. There was the mosaic clock, on the wall above the table, with its Hebrew numbers and its pretty pattern of blue and white tiles, a gift from Lazar years ago; surrounding it were squares and ovals of lighter wallpaper, marking the places where there had once been photographs of her family and pictures, nicely framed, that she had cut out of magazines. She had taken them all down; she had taken down everything from her kitchen walls except the clock. This she had done nearly two years ago already, not long after Sol had gone. And not only in the kitchen. In the living room and in the bedroom too there were these pale shapes. In the bedroom she had left nothing hanging, and in the living room there was one thing, something new: a painting by that man— who could remember his name? Schwartz? Shapiro? Schaeffer?— who painted in a minute or two such beautiful pictures (with tissue, Sammy said, and not paintbrushes). It was a picture of a rabbi, this one. Sammy had bought it for her at a hotel in the mountains, where the painter was making his fast paintings in the lobby and selling them right away to the person who offered him the highest bid. "I knew you'd love it, Mama," Sammy had said, "so I just kept bidding." And she did like it; she liked it very much. It was large and bright—it made the room a little cheerful. She had directed him to hang it for her on the wall above the sofa, where it covered up some of the faded places where other pictures had once hung. Still, all around it there were more ghost-shapes, more outlines of what used to be.

For some time now, she had been stripping down her apartment. First she had removed the framed photographs of children and grandchildren; then came the magazine pictures. But she had still felt unsatisfied. She had begun then to pack china into boxes, each piece wrapped in layers against harm, tucked within yellowed newsprint pages of the *Forward*. When she was through with the dishes, cups and bowls, platters, cake plates, saucers, she left the kitchen and began to dig through other cabinets and drawers she had not peeked into in many years. She searched all three rooms. How much she had accumulated! She herself couldn't believe it. She set up piles of things in corners, and when visitors came she offered them what she had. "Do you want your parents' wedding album?" she would ask, or, "Could you use this sugar bowl?" "How about a silver ashtray? Or this blender—take it, please, I never use a blender." Sometimes they took, sometimes not. She could tell it made them uncomfortable, either way. From time to time one of her children would ask her, "Mama, why are you doing this?" She would look up to see him staring at the naked shelves that were built right into the walls in a corner of the living room, where gilt-edged plates and statuettes and little enamel and ivory boxes had once stood.

"Getting ready," she would answer, and wave away further questions. If she was in a bad mood, she might even say, "What I do is what I do. It's not for you or any other children to judge." And if this was met with a protest, she would be firm: "Take what you want. If you don't want, don't take." If her mood was a little better, she might shake her head and say, "Don't you want this nice statue? Or this pretty china box you liked so much when you were little? How about this picture of yourself? Just look at the frame—you won't find a frame like this today."

Exactly what she was doing, she wasn't sure. She only knew that she couldn't bear all these *things* anymore. The framed photographs she knew by heart—the class pictures of her children, the one of Myra at her graduation from high school, all those important pictures commemorating important events—and she couldn't look at them any longer; they bored her. They *were* boring, she knew that. Even Rachel, who so loved photographs, had no interest in these. They now stood in a high stack beside the sofa, waiting for someone to take them away. She didn't want them around, any more than she wanted the rest of the things—the knickknacks, *tchotchkes*, all the junk she used to think was so nice. The clutter drove her mad. It wasn't a *good* clutter. She was too old for so many things.

Besides, she knew something about all these things. When she died they would be given away, given away or thrown away, or given away and then thrown away, and she couldn't stand the thought of this. It made her want to tear her hair out to think of it. So, in this way, she could decide for herself—who would get what. And if she offered something—a lamp to her niece Sophia, say, of whom she was fond, which after careful consideration seemed an appropriate pairing of object and person—and it was refused, at least she had the satisfaction of knowing that one person who might have thrown it away if it had been given to her after her own death (after Myra, perhaps, had thought, "Oh, this is just the thing to give to Sophia, who Mama always liked so much") was eliminated as a beneficiary for the item. She would think, then, of who else might want it, and she would try that person out. Slowly, slowly, she was going to get rid of everything. There would be nothing haphazard about the distribution of her belongings, not while she had control of it. She would not have anything go to the wrong person and be discarded; she had worked too hard for everything she had.

Yes, she thought, and she had worked too hard to allow anyone to get away with *taking* what was hers. She sighed and rubbed her forehead with the rough tips of her fingers. You're not getting anywhere, Rivke, she told herself. Figure this out. You may not be an educated woman, but you're a smart one. You knew how to save a dime; you knew to bring up your children. Just think. Sit still and think.

But though she sat and thought, nothing came to her. The TV bleated its pitch of company—a commercial now, all strident declarations and laughter—and she studied it for a moment; a family sat around a kitchen table. As she watched, it occurred to her that she ought to eat something. The day was beginning to slip away, and she had not yet had her breakfast.

This happened often. She couldn't understand where her

days went—the hours jumped by her so. She tilted her head from side to side, as if to let the dreaminess drain from it. She had to rouse herself from her stupor of sitting and daydreaming. All right: breakfast. Some tea, she thought. This might help. Tea and oatmeal . . . if she could just bestir herself to prepare it. And then what? To keep the day from flying by her altogether she had to plan something to do—she could not simply sit here dreaming and nodding in front of the TV.

She tried to think what she might do. Crochet? No. Even the simplest projects—and these were what she was reduced to: scarves, sashes, plain straight lines—required a certain precision for which she had not the patience today. She could take a nap—but this was a thought that held no appeal. She was weary, not sleepy. If only someone would come over, she could send him down for a paper. She hadn't seen a paper in days, or maybe a week—she could not be sure. Amos generally brought both papers when he came, the *Post* and the *Forward* too. It was good to have a paper in the house; it helped her keep track of time. Sol used to buy the *Forward* every day, and from cover to cover he would read it. She herself had never had the patience to read except for the *Bintel Briefe* column. That, she had always enjoyed—such problems people had, which they were willing to put in the paper where anyone could see them. Sol, however, had read every article, every word, and in the years since his retirement he had fallen into the habit of hovering in the kitchen while she fixed supper, reading bits of the paper aloud to her. She paid attention with only half a mind; she would tell him to leave her be. "Oh, but just listen to this!" he would cry. His voice would go high and thin, he was so excited. He'd read her a paragraph and ask, "So? What do you think of this? What is your opinion?"

Alone, for her the paper wasn't really necessary. The print was too small for her to read except with much difficulty, and she got all the news she needed from the television, anyway.

She squinted at the set now—a different family, another

kitchen. The woman was beaming. Women were always beam-ing in commercials. Why so happy? It was a mystery. For such mysteries as this she also had no patience today. She looked away and then down the length of the kitchen, and as her gaze came to the telephone she realized that she was wishing for a call from Rachel. Don't be foolish, she told herself. Ra-chel was busy; she never called in the daytime. But still her gaze rested there, as if her eyes could force the phone to ring. Then, suddenly, it did, and Rivke, astonished, stared at it. It couldn't be. For a moment she did not budge. Then, moving more quickly than usual, she pulled herself up. She was out of breath when she reached the phone.

"Yes? Hello?"

"Is Ethel there?" A male voice, accented with Russian.

Rivke's heart leapt in fear. "Who is this?"

"Who is *this*? Is Ethel there?"

"Who is this, please?" She tried to keep the tremor out of her voice. Be reasonable, she told herself. What is to fear? It is only the telephone, nothing. But there was something terri-fying about the unfamiliar voice so intimate in her ear.

"What number is this?"

Oh, of course. She exhaled and for a second she was si-lent, waiting for feeling to catch up with fact—for relief to come. No, it would be minutes yet. Her heart still pounded furiously as she said, "I'm sorry. You have dialed the wrong person."

Her shoulders hunched, head bowed, she lumbered back to the table. This did not happen often, but it happened often enough, and it never failed to upset her. Even after fear gave way to relief, a thought remained which was difficult to shake and which made her angry: the thought that anyone who chose to could reach her. Anyone! Any stranger! How could such a thing be? Why, she was *a sitting duck. An easy mark.*

As these phrases, learned from the television, came to her mind, her anger began slowly to subside. Disappointment, however, crept in to take its place. So it had not, after all, been Rachel calling; there was still no one for her to talk to.

Also, she was worn out. Moving so quickly was bad for her, it put a strain on her heart; and as she seated herself she placed her hand over her chest, taking measure of the slowing flutter that was like the wing-beating of a frail bird hidden there. This reminded her that it was time—past time—to change her nitroglycerine patch. It was fortunate that she had remembered; sometimes she forgot all day. Once again she rose from the table, thinking as she did: Up and down, all day long, it's too much for me.

In the bedroom she applied a new patch, and while she was at it she thought she might as well get dressed. This was a long process, which required much sitting and standing as she shrugged off her bathrobe and slowly pulled on underpants and pale rose-colored slacks, slid her arms into a pink blouse and a white cardigan trimmed with shiny braid—one she had made herself, years ago, when she could still accomplish such magic with needles, yarn, silver thread—and painstakingly worked the buttons. This was one of her few real chores. There was only dressing in the morning, and applying the patch over her heart three times daily. Only these things, nothing else. You would think—she often thought—it would be difficult to get through all the rest of the hours of the day, with no real work to be done. In fact, the opposite was true. Time raced by her as it never had when she was young and busy, when she had had too many things to do in a day. *Then* she had felt time hanging on her, waiting to be used. Restlessly she would work her way through what had to be done—and what had to be done was endless. The *day* was endless; it went on and on. Sometimes it seemed to her she might become trapped in a single day forever.

She had been so impatient for her life "to begin." And what had she meant by this? She found it hard to think of it now without mocking herself. Though busy, always, with-

32

out an instant to call her own, she had been secretly preoccupied with the question of when the real business of her life would get under way. While working—*like a dog,* she thought now (and then she thought: *no, harder by far than a dog. What then? Like a horse? A machine, a slave?*)—she looked to the life ahead of her: so much time ahead, years too many to count; she wondered how she might live it. Oh, the years she had spent—*spent,* she thought, yes, gave out, wasted—waiting for her life to begin in earnest!

And now look what had happened. She had not been paying attention. She had not noticed that her life *had* begun; that it was moving along; was running out. Her whole life had gone by, she felt now, as if it were a matter of minutes only. So quick! And every day it sped up more, it moved by her faster, faster. Day after day, she would turn around and discover that an hour was gone; blink, and another hour had vanished. If she sat dozing in the kitchen, when her eyes opened she would find that hours had been swallowed up, light had turned to dark, mid-day to mid-evening. Her days slipped from her so quickly she would often lose track of an entire week. No, she thought, there was no problem with passing the time. What was difficult was getting hold of it—stopping it—using it. For it would not be caught. It would not stay still long enough for her to decide what she wanted to do with it.

As she sat now on her bed, resting after the ordeal of getting dressed, a thought came to her that surprised her and filled her with shame. *I don't know what to do with my life,* she thought. And it seemed to her that she had to tell this to someone.

And suppose she were to do that! Crazy, such a thing to hear from an old woman. As if there were any life left with which to do.

So, Rivke, look what has happened. This she told herself harshly. *Some joke.* She had not been paying attention, she had been busy otherwise. Now she could see what was what but it was too late. Nine decades she had lived already, a long life for which she was supposed to be grateful. "All the time in the world"—these words went through her mind and they disgusted her. *Time?* she thought. *Time is my enemy.*

She sat thinking this over. "So," she murmured, "here is a fact to face. This is what has come to pass." She was surprised at herself: How was it that she had not seen this before now? Time had turned on her, it had become her enemy—and she had nothing with which to do battle against it; she had nothing at all.

2

Where *had* all the years gone? Rivke asked herself.

She had returned to the kitchen, where she sat with a cup of tea and a bowl of cooling oatmeal for which she had no appetite. She toyed with her teacup and spoon, tapping out no rhythm, spoon against cup, running her thumb slowly along the cup's gold-banded rim, tipping the cup until the tea was in danger of spilling.

When the children were young, and in school all day, she had been busy with washing and sweeping and cooking and sewing—and always, all the while, she had felt that she *could* be doing something else. It was a matter only of choosing to do something—anything, something different. This was what she had told herself. "Later," she'd thought. "Later. Not now." Hypnotized herself! What was "later"? It was the time that she imagined stretched out before her, suspended on the air like something she could reach out and stroke—grab hold of if she chose to. She never chose, however. She told herself she might, but that was all. Daydreams only: thoughts, no action.

Oh, once—she recalled this clearly—she had almost done something. It was a sudden thing; it flew into her head and stuck there one morning while she stood kneading bread. She stopped abruptly, floured fists in midair, so struck was she by the idea that had come to her. She would go to night school to learn to read and write in English! The plan excited her terribly; she felt she could not bear to keep it to herself for the hours until Sol came home. And what a state she worked herself into, waiting: dropped and shattered a mixing bowl, howled in imitation of the children as they screamed, sang loudly in English a song from the radio (frightening the children, who were not accustomed to this noise; she had no voice for singing) while she washed clean the breadboard. She was not herself for those hours. Then—finally—came Sol, through the door and first to the closet to put away his coat, his hat, then to the table to pour out his glass of *shnaps*—his one drink which he took each day at this time—and take it in a single swallow. She waited for him to set down the shotglass, to seat himself at the table and run his hands through his hair—already sparse, then—sigh his gladness to be home, and ask her, "*Vos makhstu?*" She, trembling, wiped her hands on her apron, hesitated for an instant in which she swallowed the words of her customary reply—"Not bad, not good"—and instead took a step toward him, and in a rush—too much of a rush, she thought for years afterwards—told him her idea.

"Absolutely not," he said. He spoke matter-of-factly. Very calm. Did he before he spoke first pause to consider? Did he bestow upon her so much as a look of apology? Perhaps a smile, signifying sympathy? No. Nothing. Absolutely not, he said. How perfectly she remembered! It might have happened yesterday, so sharp was it in her mind. First of all, it's for a wife to be home at night. Second of all—he shrugged—end of discussion.

Still (foolish!) for a few days she hoped he would change his mind. She waited for him to reconsider. She had daydreams in which he sat her down and explained that having thought it over he regretted speaking so hastily, wanted only the best for her, et cetera. At the end they held hands in the kitchen after the children were asleep and discussed the possibility of his attending night school as well, on alternate nights perhaps.

She waited; she did not herself bring up the subject.

Three days, however, passed, and at the end of this period she lost her patience. While washing dishes after supper, stealing glances at him at the table reading, she felt that if she had to keep silent for even another minute her frustration would burst in her like the bag of waters. "Why 'absolutely not'?" she asked him suddenly. He looked up from his paper and this time his expression was not so placid. "Rivke," he said—and in the way he pronounced her name she understood that he was angry—"this is impossible." But *why* impossible? she wanted to know. It would be only two, maybe three hours that she would be out of the house in the evening. Not even every evening. What was so impossible? She would leave supper already prepared for him and the children. She would even set it out on the table—she would leave him nothing to do. She would come home directly, immediately, after class; she would not stop to gossip (this she said hoping—and failing—to get a laugh from him).

He did not raise his voice—he never raised his voice; he was a mild man, quiet—but, oh, how easy a matter it was to sniff out his fury! In his eyes (such pale, pale blue eyes he had had, her husband, like tinted crystal), which narrowed until all that could be seen was a speck of their faint color; in the grip of his hands on the edges of his paper; in the tight form of his mouth as he opened it to speak, it was apparent to Rivke what was what. Furious! And yet his speech was in fact softer even than usual—it was his way when angry—and the words came from him as if he were counting them and it cost him to give them up: so carefully, so slowly. What he said in this stiff, reluctant way, as if words were pennies dropped one at a time into a palm, was that it was unfair—unreasonable, *not right*—for her to expect him to stay with the children in the evening after his long day at the factory. "This is your work," he said. "Not mine. I have my work. Yours is yours."

"But what work are we speaking of?" she said. "There will *be* no work. I will take care of all that needs to be done, I will leave you nothing. This I promise you."

Silence for a moment; when he spoke again it was in a

voice that was softer *still*. He reminded her that at her insistence he had long ago given up "running out" in the evening; he suggested that he might take up once again his old habit. "If you can run out as you like, why not I?" This infuriated her, as he had of course known it would. The "running out" to which he referred had been an ugly business during the first year of their marriage, when he used to vanish right from work and for hours play cards and drink beer, often gambling away half his wages before she saw them.

She argued with him, but in the end she lost. She had known in her heart that she would lose—or so she came to think in later years. How could she have won this argument? It was his right to demand that she remain at home; this she felt to be true. She felt too, however, that it was a right he did not have to exercise; that he had chosen to do so she could not forgive.

Even now she did not forgive him. Fifty years had passed since that time—or perhaps it was more than fifty years; it was hard to keep track of a thing like this—but years alone could not take such a bitterness from her; they could only bury it so that she had to dig for it—though she did not, it was true, have to dig very deeply—to feel it once again. And when she felt it, she felt it as if it were new, recent! As if no time had passed! Sitting at her kitchen table, so many years after that evening when he had told her "absolutely not," she trembled—this was how strongly her old anger returned to her.

To this day she could read only enough English to manage the simple language of the *Post* or the *Daily News*—and, at that, not even every article, and not even every word of those articles which she was able to read—and she could write in English hardly at all. For this, could she forgive him? This was the one thing she held against him in seventy-two years of marriage. Only this. In every other way he had been a good husband. Stubborn, maybe, but that was only his character; she couldn't fault him for that. People were what they were.

Oh, naturally she could have wished for him to be a little sterner with the children, but it hadn't been in his nature. They could kick and punch each other, tear at each other's hair, right under his nose, and he would only turn the pages of his newspaper and sigh—more than once she had seen this happen. Well, this could not be helped. He could not have disciplined them; he would not have known how. He was a very gentle person, a different sort from her. Not that she was not herself a gentle person. It pained her greatly to scold her children, to punish them. But it was left to her and it was a necessary thing—and she, unlike Sol, could always manage to do what was essential, however unpleasant. In any case, he saw so little of the children, if he had been the one responsible for their punishment, this would have amounted to his only relation with them. As it was, there existed a great tenderness between father and children. The children, in fact, adored him. Sometimes (though she would admit this to no one) it hurt her to see how devoted they were to him, when they were so often angry with her. Naturally they were angry with her! She was the one to say no to this, no to that. It was she who sent them to bed without supper; it was she who threatened them with the strap. Sol they only saw to get a kiss from him, or a penny, or a kind, absent-minded word. In the morning he left before they awoke; in the evening he returned too tired to do anything but eat his supper and look at his paper for an hour before going to sleep. *She* was up each night until two o'clock, three o'clock, mending and tidying and thinking. Finally she would drag herself to bed, but once there she lay awake. Sometimes Sol would half awaken in the night and stroke her arms, muttering, "Rivkeleh, you should be sleeping." Simple for him to say! But anything could happen while she slept. She had to keep vigilant; everything depended on her. It was up to her alone to keep the house in order, to prepare meals without forgetting who was willing to eat what, to stop the children from smacking and biting each other, to repair the clothes they tore to pieces playing after school. She had to keep an eye on the children at all times. Even as she cooked Sol's evening meal she had to pay attention to what was going on in the living room, for at any moment Reuben and Sammy might begin to fight, Ruby sitting on his younger brother's chest and pounding his head against the floor while Myra, the baby, screamed, "Ma, they're killing each other!"

How could she rest? If she didn't watch closely over Amos, he would disappear to make some mischief somewhere—beat up a smaller boy, steal oranges from the man who sold fruit on the corner of Fifth Street. She would have to go after him and apologize for whatever he had done, then rush home to see to the others, and who knew what they might have been up to in her absence?

She was forever running. She ran to the school to talk to teachers who sent home notes the children had to help her read: Amos was playing hooky, Lazar needed glasses, Reuben hadn't done his homework for two weeks. Problems, always problems. At twelve Amos insisted he wasn't going to be *bar mitzve*; at sixteen Ruby wanted to quit school. There was a period of months during which Sammy refused to have anything to do with the others. Always something. At six, Myra (Myra, her angel, a child good as gold, who had never given her a moment's trouble until then) began suddenly to stutter. What do you do with a child who stutters? There was no one to ask. Today, Rivke thought, one would have only to turn on the television: sooner or later this would be spoken of. But in those years? She knew that something had to be done. It made her frightened and angry to think that a child of hers might live her life talking this way. Myra was an American child; English was hers by birth. She was entitled. *Proper* English, English as it was supposed to be spoken—not this crippled string of words that caught on the child's tongue and stuck there waiting to drop, then dropped at the wrong time. She thought and thought about it, and finally she told Myra, "Talk to me right or I'm not going to answer you." For weeks Myra followed her around the apartment, tugging at her apron and whining, begging her mother to speak to her; every word she spoke sent a sharp angry flash like a needle's work through Rivke. She would turn her face away, hiding her feelings from the child, and say, with careful innocence, "Did I hear a noise? I wonder what could be that funny noise? I maybe am hearing things." Then one day Myra appeared in the doorway to the kitchen, half-hidden in the early-morning darkness there, whispering, "Mama, may I have some cereal please?" Rivke had so grown accustomed to not responding to her daughter's voice she almost failed to catch the significance of this perfect sentence. When after a minute it dawned on her, she had to fight an impulse to rush to the child and gather her up in her arms, crying out her relief and gratitude—would this not have embarrassed her daughter? She took hold of herself and managed to say, calmly, "Of course, darling, come sit down here and I'll make some cream of wheat."

And that was it, finished: no more stuttering. For years no more stuttering. Now, when from time to time she fell again into that old habit, Rivke knew she was not supposed to become angry. It was not her responsibility any longer. Myra was past fifty, past changing. This in itself of course was amazing. Past fifty! How was it, then, that even now she could conjure up the child Myra standing big-eyed and uncertain in the shadows of the doorway? As if it were days ago that this had been, not years—not decades. Clear as daylight she could see her coming slowly into the kitchen, a skinny, stoop-shouldered little girl with great dark eyes like Rivke's own mother, Mina, for whom the child had been named, the long black braids dangling from just below each ear. Her only daughter, her youngest! Her baby. No more: only in memory. But so clearly she could see this!

Not only this. How often, after all, over the years since the children had all grown up and married, had she glanced up from the table and imagined she saw one or another of them there before the entrance to the kitchen? And not only her children. Now that Sol was gone she would look up too quickly and see *him* there, tipping his head at her and smiling like an imp, calling, "Rivkeleh, come see what I brought you," and leaning down into the shopping cart to pull out some nonsense—Hershey's chocolate, graham crackers, ice cream.

These tricks of her memory—how they plagued her! She would sit here at the table in the kitchen and think she heard Sol rustling his *Forward* in the living room. At dawn, restless, she would go to the kitchen for a glass of water and for an instant see him standing by the table, head bent over his prayer-book, *davening* as he had done each morning at this hour for so many years. What she saw, she told herself, was what she was used to seeing. Likewise what she heard. But nearly four decades after her youngest had grown too old for courtyard games, how did it happen that she would still sometimes believe she heard her children taunting each other in the court-yard below? She would have to keep herself from leaning out the kitchen window to hush them as she used to. She would tell herself, "Rivke, stop your foolishness. There is no one here but you. You are all alone now. Everything has changed."

Everything had changed—everything. Everything! Look at my kitchen, she thought—and with a feeling of helplessness she looked around her. Here was a room which had once been full of life, activity. And how it used to shine from all her scrubbing and scraping! Now look at it. It was dingy, it was greasy-looking—terrible. The oilcloth that covered the floor curled up at the edges and was layered with dirt. And it had been so beautiful when she'd bought it! White and red flowers, a happy pattern. Sol, for at least ten years, had been after her to replace it. "Rivke, it's old," he said, "and it makes you un-happy to look at it." But she pointed out that it would be a waste of money to put new oilcloth down unless they painted the kitchen first. "So we'll paint," he said. But who had strength to prepare for painters? The whole apartment needed painting, not only the kitchen, and what a job that would be. "When I feel a little stronger," she told him, "then we'll paint. *Then* we'll buy a new piece of oilcloth." She had put it off and put it off—and now? Now it was altogether impossible. Also pointless. For whom should she fuss? The answer to this was nobody. Pointless! But it pained her nonetheless to see what her apartment had become, when she used to keep it so nice— everything in its place and clean, beautiful. And yet what could she do? It was too much for her. Even to sweep was exhausting now, and to sweep in any case was only to move around the dirt. Once in a while she took up a rag and beat dust from the furniture into the air—and then she would sneeze all night. But more than this? To scrub or to mop a floor required strength. Could she perhaps push the vacuum cleaner around the rooms? Ha! She could not bend to fit the parts of the vacuum cleaner together.

So what could she do, then? Nothing—there was nothing she could do. She could only try not to notice the condition of the rooms in which she lived. And how was it possible not to notice? To this problem there was no solution, only the temporary remedy of closing her eyes.

Which was what she did now, giving in at last to the weariness that had been creeping up on her all morning. She was entitled to a little rest, she thought—and at this thought she even managed a smile. A little rest, it seemed to her, was the least of what she was entitled to.

Rachel called in the evening, as usual, shortly after eight o'clock. Rivke was at the table mending a blouse when the telephone rang; it was a blouse she had not worn in years and had always disliked, a gift from a daughter-in-law (which one, she couldn't recall). An old lady's blouse, high-necked, the milky yellow color of something spoiled, trimmed with false lace.

One would have to look for a long time to find a blouse so ugly, Rivke reflected as she worked. But this was unimportant; it was not real work, this loose-stitched, clumsy closing of an inch of seam that had parted long ago: it was only meant to be an excuse to keep herself still while she waited for Rachel's call.

"For more than an hour I've been waiting," she told her granddaughter when finally the call had come.

"Is that so?" Rachel said. "Tell me, when have I ever called before eight o'clock?"

"This is what you call an answer? It's nice to keep an elderly woman waiting?"

Rachel groaned—a mock-groan only; this was a familiar exchange between them. "All right, then, would you like me to call earlier from now on?"

"No, *meydeleh*," Rivke said. "Of course not. What then would I have to look forward to?"

"To something better than my phone calls, I should hope."

"Is there something better? I should look forward to a night of dancing? Come, tell me about your day. You're staying home tonight? Or you're going out later? It's still early for you, no?"

"One thing at a time. Tell me first how you're feeling."

"How I'm feeling? What's to tell, how should I be feeling? Old is old, there's nothing to say. What I'm interested to hear about is you."

"Has anyone ever told you that you're a very difficult person?"

"Never," Rivke said. "Come on, tell me, how was your day? Tell me some good news, something happy."

As Rachel began her recitation of the day's events, Rivke, holding the receiver tightly to her ear, the long cord trailing behind her, returned to the table and settled herself there to listen in comfort. Rachel spoke first of her new part-time job at the art gallery, where she had spent the morning answering the phone and typing letters; for Rivke's amusement she imitated the voices of both the gallery's owner, Alexandra ("SoHo yuppie," she said. "Remind me to explain that later"), and a young artist named Raphael ("Or so he says") who was to have his work exhibited at the gallery next month. "*Artist* is a term I use loosely here, however," Rachel said. "What this fellow paints is cartoons, giant cartoons on giant canvases, lots of bright colors."

"That is art?"

"I wonder myself. Depends on what you decide to call art, I suppose."

"But someone has decided already that this is called art?" Rivke was pleased with herself; she delighted in this sort of talk—although, frequently, while on the phone with Rachel, she worried she would become dangerously overexcited; even now she felt her heartbeat and her breathing quickening.

"Neo-expressionist art," Rachel said. "Remind me to explain that too." Then, switching voices back and forth, she recreated an argument that had occurred this morning between the gallery owner and the painter. "Two *big* egos," she said when Rivke stopped laughing, "and two tiny little intellects. Oy, Grandma, you should have seen them. Picture this: There's Alexandra, all four-foot-ten of her plus permanent and pearls, getting madder and madder—and trying not to raise her voice, you see, because she doesn't *believe* in raising her voice—and here's Raphael, this very creepy, dissipated-looking character, unshaven of course, skinny like you wouldn't believe and maybe six and a half feet tall, in magenta hip-huggers and a biker jacket and plaid hightops, and they're practically *spitting* at each other."

"Tell me what is *dissipated.*"

"Used up. Worn out. You know?"

"Ah, yes, I know. So then what happened?"

"Then it was noon and I left. You know, Rivke, it's a crazy world."

"Ha! You're telling me?"

Rachel next described the afternoon's picture-taking expedition to Washington Square Park, where she had spent over an hour watching and photographing a father and daughter. "Oh, they were lovely—wonderful," she said. "I can't begin to tell you. He kept collecting her at the bottom of the sliding pond: he'd scoop her up and she'd wrap herself around him like a monkey, just for a minute, then he'd let her down and she'd run around the back of the slide to start again."

"And then? After the park?"

"After the park . . . let's see. . . . Oh, I know. I stopped for coffee at the Peacock—first I bought the paper—then after I had my coffee I shopped for groceries. Then I came home, cleaned up a little, had a bowl of soup. Spent a couple of hours in the darkroom—and here I am. Maybe it was three hours in the darkroom. Anyway, I accomplished plenty. Today I have no complaints—a good day's work, all told."

"So, why do you sound surprised? Why shouldn't you have a good day?"

"Why is right." Rivke could see the shrug, the tossed hair—so dark almost black, and thick also, wild with curls that swung like lengths of rope: exactly like the hair of Rivke's own youth. "Some days are better than others, however. And some days—I might go so far as to say—are altogether terrible. Today happened not to be one of them. Not yet, I should add—it's not over, *kineahora*." Rivke heard the rap of knuckles on wood.

"Rucheleh, there is no reason why all your days should not be good ones."

"Rivkeleh, there are plenty of reasons."

"If this is true . . ." Rivke paused, considering whether she should say what she had in mind.

"Uh-oh, I know what's coming. Do me a favor and don't say it, okay?"

". . . this is *because*," Rivke said, although she knew she shouldn't, "you are all alone."

"Oh, Rivke, Rivke," Rachel said. "Why do you do this to me? Tell me, is it necessary? You in the mood for a fight or what?"

"Is it so terrible," Rivke said mildly, "that I wish for you to have someone? I'm wishing you only love, companionship, happiness. Love, Rucheleh! That's not so bad, is it?"

"No, it's not so bad. It's nice, it's wonderful. It's only irrelevant. I *like* being alone. I like *living* alone." She spoke in a singsong; this too was familiar business between them. "And anyway I've found, in my vast experience, that most men aren't worth the paper they're printed on."

"All I ask," Rivke said, "is that before I join Papa —"

"No, no, no, *enough*. No more of this. I promise that when I find the right man you'll be the first to know, okay? On to another subject now. You must have *something* you can tell me. Gossip, maybe? A family scandal? A good dream last night?"

So — it was time. Rivke felt a sudden small explosion of tension within her; it began at once to spread, moving through her so rapidly she became dizzy. As if it were carried by her very blood! she thought. Through veins, to the head. A lucky thing she was not on her feet. "Yes, I have something to tell you. Not good news." She cleared her throat. "Listen. The beads I've been saving for you?"

"Beads." For an instant — it was not even an instant, it was perhaps a small portion of an instant — there was silence. Then: "Oh, yes, sure, of course. The black ones. From the dress. You were going to make a necklace."

"It's too late now for necklaces, *mamaleh*. The beads are gone. Someone took them."

"What do you mean, 'gone'?"

"Gone means gone."

"Gone, just like that?"

"Just like that. Someone took them and left me the empty box as a present."

"Oh, Grandma, are you sure? Who would do such a thing?"

"Who, exactly? Who comes here?"

"Wait, wait, let's just think for a minute. How can they just be *gone*?"

"How? What means 'how'? You know how."

"But who would take them?"

"Who? Who comes?"

"I don't know. Me. Ma. The uncles, their wives. A couple of cousins, I guess. Debbie?"

"Good, that's right."

Briefly she was silent again. "Ah." Quietly. "You think Debbie took them."

"No," Rivke said. She had to smile. How like her this child was! And who else was so like her? No one! Not one of her own children! She could not understand it. How was it that in this family of so many—in this family which she herself was responsible for creating—only one child, one child of one child of her own, seemed truly to be *of* her?

"Think, Rucheleh. Think. Who else comes?"

"Mark and Rhonda," Rachel said. Then: "Oh, no, Grandma, Mark and Rhonda? You don't think Mark and Rhonda took them?"

"Your brother?" Rivke felt offended. "My daughter's son?"

"His wife, then. Rhonda."

Rivke did not speak. She wanted to give Rachel time to think.

"So you think it's her."

Still Rivke said nothing.

"Oh, Grandma." A lengthy, noisy sigh filled Rivke's ear. "Oh, boy. What now? What are you going to do?"

"I don't know, *mamaleh*. What do you think I should do? Should I say something? This is the main thing. I'm worried Mark will be angry."

"He'll be angry all right. Grandma, I don't know, I just wonder. . . . What makes you so sure it's her?"

"It's somebody," Rivke said dryly. "Somebody took them. They didn't just walk away by themselves."

"But why would she take them? For what reason?"

"For what reason? There are plenty of reasons for everything. This you should know, you're a smart girl. People do what they do."

"Maybe so, but this is. . . . Oh, I don't know. I just wonder. . . ." In the pause that followed, with only their breathing between them, Rivke felt suddenly endangered. *Just speak*, she thought. *Say what you have to say.* But why should she feel afraid? Afraid of what? Rachel of all people would not harm her. This was something she knew; this was something she should hold on to, not forget. Still, waiting for the silence to end, she was anxious—she was full of dread. And then at last Rachel spoke. Hesitantly, she said, "Grandma, it's just that I wonder if you think there might be a chance—any chance at all, even a small, small chance—that you took the beads out of the box, planning to start work on stringing them, and put them—"

"Rachel, darling," Rivke interrupted, "*please*. This is just not true. I wish it were true. Don't you think I wish? Don't you think I wish I had the beads still? I never touched them."

"Well."

"Well?" Rivke was trembling.

"Maybe. . . ." Rachel's breathing was loud in Rivke's ear. "I don't know. I don't know. Maybe they'll turn up."

"Turn up? You think who took them is going to put them back?" But she didn't wait for Rachel's answer; she was distracted by an idea that had just now come to her. "All right, Rucheleh," she said. "You're tired. You should go to sleep. We can talk more another time, yes?"

"Yes, of course we can. I'll call you tomorrow."

"Good. Good night, I love you."

"I love you, too," Rachel said. "Sweet dreams."

Rivke clattered the receiver down. A good idea! And Rachel had unknowingly given it to her. She could simply say, in Rhonda's presence, "Oh, I miss those beads that were taken from me. I only wish that whoever took them would put them back. I wouldn't say anything, I would be so happy to have them back again." Of course! This was the best way to handle it, no question. She would wait until Mark and his wife's next visit; she would mention casually that the beads she had been saving were gone; and then after a while, when they had come to talk of other things, she would say, "How I miss those beads that I for so long was keeping!" Yes, this was what she would say. She would speak very quietly, not to frighten the girl. "Oh," she would say, "how I wish that the person who took those beads would put them back." She would say this, she would speak gently. Perhaps then the girl would return them.

She was preoccupied with this plan for the rest of the evening. In its way it was a soothing thing to think about—the simplicity of it especially pleased and calmed her; it seemed to her it could not be simpler. All that was required was for her to state what she felt—nothing else; then she had only to be still and see what would come of it. She might not even wait for a visit; for who knew how long it would be before this came to pass? Months, it could be. No, there was no need to wait. She could say what she had to say on the telephone, the next time Mark called. She would hear from him soon, she was certain; for more than a week to elapse between his calls was unusual. She could say what she had to say, and hope that he would repeat it to his wife. And probably he would, Rivke thought. Husbands repeated. And it could be that this alone would do it—in any case it would not hurt to try.

With a course of action in her mind, she felt relieved; and as she prepared herself for sleep, removing her clothes and folding them, removing and rinsing her teeth, spreading out a sheet and stacking up pillows at both ends of the sofa—a stack for her head and a stack for her feet—and filling the hot water bag, it occurred to her that she might even be able to get a true rest tonight—she was that much at ease; she felt almost contented.

It was even possible, she thought while settling into position on the sofa, that she would sleep through the night altogether. And why not? Certainly she deserved a night's sleep for once. She shrugged to herself as she pulled the blanket up around her neck and closed her eyes. For a moment she lay quietly. Then—so softly she could hardly hear herself, and without having decided to do so—she began to sing a little. The song she found herself singing in a whisper (as if, she thought, she were afraid someone else might hear her) was the song she used to sing to Rachel, to put her to sleep when she was a child; it had been sung to her by her own grandmother, Ruchel, in *her* childhood, in the old country—the song was *Rozhinkes mit Mandlen*.

Unter Yidele's vigele
Shteyt a klor veys tsigele.

As she sang, a picture of the little goat, the *tsigele*, came into her mind, and this made her smile—this, and the memory of tiny Rachel asking her, "And what is a goat?" She was very young; she had never seen a goat or a picture of a goat. The white *tsigele*, under the cradle, the *vigele*—these things Rivke could see as she lay in the dark; and also Rachel, Rachel half asleep listening as Rivke sat beside her and sang to her and rubbed her small shoulders and back. And also—suddenly—Ruchel's face near hers. She saw her, her grandmother, with her eyes closed as she leaned down to sing into Rivke's ear, her deep, beautiful voice and her small, strong hands working together to put Rivke to sleep: the voice filling up her ear and taking over so that nothing else was in her mind; the fingers kneading her back the way they kneaded the dough each morning for the bread she would sell that day.

Rivke sang now hardly knowing she was singing. She sang until she came to the end, and when she did—when she came to the words *Shlof zhe, Yidele, shlof*, the place in the song when she used to stroke her granddaughter's hair and add in English, "Sleep now, sleep"—she sighed deeply and turned her face to the pillow. It was only another instant, and then she was asleep herself.

3

So much noise. Rivke shook her head at the TV. She continued to watch for a few minutes, frowning, and then with a grunt reached across the table to shut off the set. "Enough screaming," she said. "Enough clapping."

Without Sol at her side in front of the big color TV in the living room, "The Price Is Right," which they had watched with pleasure for years, had ceased to entertain her. It used to be something for them to talk about: they would guess together the cost of things. But why did she bother with it still? Every day she watched, and every day she was irritated.

Well, she was not obliged to look at it, she told herself. Habits could be changed. She would leave the TV off until twelve-thirty, she decided, when "The Young and the Restless" came on. This she had always watched alone, in the kitchen; it had been Sol's time to go out to the Speedway to do the shopping. He'd had no patience with all the problems on this show. "Too much is whining" was what he used to say.

Absently, Rivke dipped her teaspoon into the mug of hot water before her on the table, and brought the spoon to her lips. The water was no longer hot. She thought she would get up, go to the stove and add water to her mug from the kettle— but even thinking of moving made her feel tired. In a minute then, she told herself. For now she had better just sit.

She was waiting for the telephone to ring. For a whole week she had been waiting—like this, not impatiently; but her patience was not endless. This morning she had begun to wonder if she would ever again hear from her grandson. Each day she rehearsed the speech she planned to make when he called—and each day when the phone rang her chest tightened and her heart began to jump in its cage of bones; but always it was someone else calling, not him. In the morning it was Myra; in the evening, Rachel. In between came calls from her sons—one one day, another the next. Also this week two grandchildren from whom she had not heard in several months surprised her with calls, and her nephew Meyer, Essie's only son, who from time to time would have an urge to talk to her, called early one morning, even before Myra. That was all.

They called, she talked. This was fine, this was what the telephone was for. What she wanted to talk about, however, she couldn't talk about. About the missing beads she could talk to nobody but Rachel. It was plain to her that no one else was interested. Myra, who had come to see her three days after she had discovered the theft, had sat listening to her talk about it for only a little while before she said, "Mama, please, you're driving me crazy with this, not to mention yourself. Try to forget about it, why don't you?"

To Myra, she had of course not said anything about Rhonda; she had only mentioned that it would be a kindness if the person who was responsible for the theft would return the beads to her. "To treat an old woman this way," Rivke said, "this seems to me a terrible thing, a shameful thing, no?" Myra's answer to this was silence, and after a moment Rivke considered it best to let the matter drop. An argument she was not looking for.

And her sons? Was this something to discuss with them? To Amos she had mentioned the disappearance of "a certain item" from her house, and he had interrupted to talk of the vacation to Florida he and Frances were planning. Her other boys Rivke did not even have to think of talking to about this—she knew better; she was not so foolish as to try.

And now the phone was ringing. *At last!* she thought. She

grasped the table to help herself up; she wobbled a little but then she was standing, and after making certain she was stable on her feet, she proceeded slowly to the telephone. "Be him," she said as she approached it. It could be him, this time. Myra she had already heard from today. Three rings, four rings—she lifted the receiver halfway through the fifth. "Yes? Who is this, please?"

"Mama, this is not a nice way to answer the phone."

Not Mark—a son. But which son? It always took a few seconds to decide. Only Amos's voice was distinctly different from the others'. "Lazar?" she guessed.

"No, Ma." Ah, the laugh. If they'd only laugh right away she'd know right away. This was Reuben. Lazar's laugh was sniffly, held in, as if he didn't want to be laughing (and who could blame him, with his troubles? A child who refused to have anything to do with him, a grandchild he had never seen—and a *farbisseneh* wife, a woman who spoke bile, not words, and who on her own without any other misfortunes occurring could have made his life a misery). Samuel, her youngest son, had a laugh that was warm but timid-sounding, nervous—afraid to laugh, this was what one heard in his laughter. But Reuben laughed like a TV game show host: loud, from his belly, with a snorting sound. He stopped this laugh now and said, "So when'll you ever learn to tell your sons apart?"

"I'm old," Rivke said. "Some things are harder now."

"Old? Come on, Mama. You're sharp as a tack. You're not old."

"I *am* old. I'm very, very old." Usually she played along with this game of Reuben's—old, young. But today she had no taste for it.

"Ah, that's nonsense, Mama." Still, he let it go. He laughed again, a smaller, quieter version this time, and he said, "So? Tell me, how are you?"

"Me?" Rivke laughed too in return, delicately. "Me, I'm just the same, like always. But *you*, Reuveleh? You're feeling all right? Everything is fine at home?"

"Well, Ma," Ruby said, "to tell you the truth, it's like this. 'Fine' is probably too much to ask for. I've got Julia and Candy here now, you know? By itself that's no picnic. And lately that lousy husband of Julia's keeps calling. It's driving Sally nuts."

Silently Rivke cursed herself for asking. She had to hear Ruby's wife's name spoken? This was a witch, this woman. Rivke did not like to think of her, not even of her name. For years – decades – she had been nothing but unpleasant to Rivke. Worse than unpleasant. Rotten. Once she had wished aloud for her death. In Rivke's presence she had said this – wished for her death! This was years ago – it was more than twenty years now since this had happened. Still, Rivke remembered it very well. Though how it was possible that the wife of a son should utter something like this she understood no better to-day than she had then. Now – oh, long ago already – Sally had decided she would have nothing more to do with Rivke. The reason for this had never been named. But as far as Rivke was concerned it was fine. Who needed to see such a *makhshey-feh*? Who needed to hear anything about a wife like this? And the daughter! Why was it necessary for them to tell her these things? Was it so necessary for her to know all this? About Ruby's girl Julia who had had her baby without a husband, and the boy (Rivke did not even know his name – not first, not last), who had decided later to marry her after all? They kept Rivke informed, she shouldn't miss anything! First no marriage, then marriage, then no marriage again because somebody had left somebody. *Ongepotchket!* No sense whatsoever. For this they called her? To tell her bad news? So much nonsense, who knew what went on? Oh, she knew, she saw it all on TV. But who needed it right in your own family?

"Ruby," she said, "let's talk about good things."

But he didn't care for that. "Well, Mama," he said, "the trouble is, there just isn't a whole lot good to talk about these days. I should tell you, we heard from Rich again."

Another one. All of Reuben's children had turned out

badly. Three children, no luck with any. And her own? She was suddenly filled with fury. Her own! They called her only to tell her their *tsuris*. "Mama, how are you?" they said. "Everything's okay? You feel all right?" Nice words to show their concern. Oh, yes, they were concerned. Some concern. *Shame*, she thought. *They should all be ashamed.*

And here was Reuben, talking, talking. "He wants us maybe to come out and see him, Ma. He's in San Diego now, he says he's doing much better. Naturally he asked for money. I knew that was coming. But you know what? This time I decided to go ahead and send him some. I figured—oh, what the hell, he's my kid, he's entitled. And he says he's doing better, a lot better."

Rivke sucked in her cheeks. What was she to say about this? What was there to say? Reuben was going to run now to see his son who had spit in his face, who poisoned himself with drugs and had no use for his family except for money— and did he ever think to come see *her*? For an ungrateful child he would run all the way to California. And for Rivke, who was alone in a place that felt no longer like a home, could he ride in the car for one hour or two?

It was not as if they didn't know how she felt. Many times she had told the children, "A home is not a home without somebody in it." Myra had an answer to this. "Don't be silly, Ma," she would say. "You're in it. You're somebody." Who had strength for such an argument? And even if she were strong enough, was it worth the effort for her to argue? Nothing would change if she did. After the funeral, after the week of *shivah* at Myra's house on Long Island, and then some time afterwards—how long she couldn't remember—of everyone looking at her too closely, they had packed her up and sent her home. Home? It wasn't a home anymore. But where else was there to go? Nowhere: nobody made her any offers. And she wasn't asking. Would she, in any case, be able to stand living with her children? Any one of them? Her sons with their crazy wives? Myra's husband always yelling?

Amos had said, "Mama, I want you to know I wish I could have you with us, but with Frances so sick herself it would be too hard on her." Hard on *her*! God should forgive her, Rivke thought, but she could not find it in her heart to feel sorry for Frances. The way she kept after Amos! Let's go here, let's go there. And always on the telephone, always shopping – she didn't know how to save a penny. She needed this, she needed that. *This* was the sickness, not the swelling of her legs or the soreness in her hips which she complained about until you wanted to scream. And Amos with his "I wish"! What was a wish? What was it worth? Could you ride the subway on a wish? And now Rivke had to laugh at herself, because how long had it been since she'd been on the subway? Or on a bus, for that matter? Or out of the apartment. As long as there was still ice on the ground, she was afraid to go out.

"Ma? Why so quiet? You still there?"

"Naturally I'm here, I'm always here. Where else should I be?" And then, wickedly, she added, "I'll be going soon enough, I promise you."

"Oh, don't talk like that, Mama. You'll outlive us all."

"Mm," Rivke said. That game. Not today.

There was an unhappy silence now. Rivke knew she had made him feel bad; she felt sorry for this. To add to her children's unhappiness was not what she wanted. They all had hard lives, she knew. They all suffered. Not one of them had married into a good family. This she had seen right away, every time. But had anyone listened to her? Ha.

"Well, Reuveleh," she said gently, "let me tell you something to make you laugh. You know that crazy woman from downstairs?"

"Which woman?"

"You know, that crazy blond woman on the second floor. She came knocking up here the other day. Nosy. She wanted to see if I was still alive."

"*Which* woman, Mama?"

57

"You know. The one with all the lipstick. She calls herself a *rebbetzin*. A *rebbetzin* she's not. You know, she used to grab Papa in the lobby—'Hello, Mister Vasilevsky, it's so nice to see you'—and she would give him a squeeze and kiss him with all that lipstick of hers. He couldn't stand it. You know what *khaloshes* means, Ruby?"

"Sure, Ma, of course I know. Disgusting."

"Ah, you still remember a few things from your old mama."

"So what did she want?"

"I told you. She wanted to see if I was dead yet." Rivke snorted out a laugh.

"Don't say things like that, Mama, please. It's bad."

Bad for who? she wanted to ask. But she behaved herself; instead she said, "All the neighbors are Russians now, Ruby, do you know that?"

"Oh, Ma," he said and sighed, "not *all.*"

"Yes. Almost all. Nobody from before is here. The *rebbetzin*, Mrs. Birnbaum from the fifth floor, that elderly woman Mrs. Rosenstein—she must be a hundred years old—and me. That's all. The rest are Russians. It's terrible. It's not the same. Not like it was." She was beginning to get excited, but Reuben made a clicking sound in his throat, a signal he was getting ready to hang up. Rivke began to talk faster to hold his attention. "They make so much noise—*klopping, klopping* day and night. And jumping on the floor—I don't know what they do. Last night I thought the ceiling was going to come down. How many do they have in those rooms upstairs, I wonder. Maybe ten, maybe more."

"They have to live somewhere, Ma."

"But here? Why here? They just come and come. It didn't used to be so easy to come. Now they come on boats, nobody stops them."

"Mama, they have to leave Russia and they have to go somewhere. You could have a little sympathy."

"For them you want me to have sympathy? *I* should have

rakhmones for the Russians when they own now the whole neighborhood? The government gives them the money to buy from who used to have stores. Now all the stores, all the restaurants, everything is owned by the Russians." She was getting overexcited, she realized, and she knew she ought to calm herself, but she was too involved now to be interested in being calm. "When I came I had *nothing*. And Papa had nothing. It was 1909 when I came to this country. I was only fourteen years old. Do you think it was easy for me? And for Papa, do you think it was easy for him? Nothing was easy for us, nothing was given to us. We worked hard; it was a difficult life. But for the Russians? For them, everything is easy. From the government they have their rent, food, nice clothes to wear—from the government they have everything. If they want *rakhmones*, this they can get from the government too." Again she heard that clicking at the other end of the line and she knew she wouldn't be able to hold him any longer. "All right, *zuneleh*. I'll let you get back to your work. I know you're busy."

"I am, Ma. You wouldn't believe how busy it is here now. And then at home, with the kid—"

"Yes, I know, I know all about kids. Go. Go ahead. I love you." She waited for the smack of a kiss into the phone, then she hung up, settling the receiver slowly into its wall cradle.

She stared at it for a moment—the black receiver with its snake of curly rubber hanging from it—and she narrowed her eyes and frowned. Ah, well, she thought. Children.

They make phone calls, they buy presents. They ruin their lives and then come crying. And she was supposed to give comfort. Again and again and again—there was no end to it. So many years of crying, so many years of comforting. And for what? So they could leave to start families of their own—and look what this had come to. Pure craziness in all of these families, craziness sprinkled over all her children's lives like salt. They couldn't take care of *their* children. Yet she had managed to take care of all of them. And now, look how life works

out, all five of them plus all their children and their grandchildren, and all of them together couldn't take care of her.

She was still a little out of breath from her talk of the Russians, and as she returned to the table she laughed mockingly
at herself—*politician! Big shot! You think you know something?
When were you last on the avenue to see those stores you talk about
so aggravated?* She shook her head. For a few minutes then,
standing at the table, she busied herself with adding water to
her mug from the kettle she had kept boiling, and squeezing
the last drops from a piece of lemon. Now she sat down, heav-
ily, tilting the chairback against the radiator. The heat was on,
at least. That was good, something to be thankful for. There
were some things for which to be thankful. She had a home—
not much of a home, it was true, and she couldn't keep it clean
now, but it was hers, as long as she paid rent.

She let her eyes droop closed. It would be nice to sleep a
little; at night she slept so badly. Naturally she slept badly, she
thought: bad nights naturally followed bad days. What were
her days? Every day of her life she had worked hard, and now
there was nothing left for her to do but watch television and
answer the phone. Was this a life?

Feh. She swatted away the thought like a fly. It was her
life, an old woman's life. There was always something to be
done. Her crocheting. Mending. She wanted to make a new
scarf for Rachel. A blanket for Amy's baby, Debbie's little
granddaughter. There was plenty to do. Sol used to laugh at
her—so busy, even when there was no one left but the two of
them. "Always fixing," he said. "Always making."

Oh, she missed him. She missed him much more than she
could have guessed she would. These last few years she had
become so easily irritated with him. She'd had to shout for
him to hear her, and he had refused to get a hearing aid. He
had said no also to her pleas that he get a stick to walk with,
he said he had no need, and yet she could see how his legs
trembled sometimes, how they failed him. In the morning

when he first woke up he could not stand on his own; she would stay in bed and watch him with one eye open—watch him leaning on the nighttable, then on the dresser, moving slowly across the room from one piece of furniture to the next. When he went out to the Speedway, or even just across the street to Mendy's for a quart of milk, she worried, afraid he'd fall. But would he get a stick? So stubborn! Impossible. And always—always—pinching and kissing, when the time for that was long over. She had to constantly shoo him away, tell him to go into the living room, read his paper, leave her be. "Pest," she would say to him. "Why are you all the time bothering me? Find something to do with yourself."

But she could not get used to his not being here. How could a person get used to this? They had been together for so long—a lifetime. He had taken her from her family, from the tumult of Leah's house, where there was no place for her and she was made crazy with all the shouting and scolding of relatives and boarders both. He had rescued her. She'd been working then making buttons in a factory for three dollars a week. "Better I should give you the three dollars and you should stay home," he told her. And then: "Better, maybe, you should marry me altogether." He himself was an orphan, the youngest of six children, two of whom had died in childhood; of the family that remained, only Etke, the eldest, who was by this time busy with a husband and children of her own, cared to have anything to do with him: the others kept their distance. When he and Rivke were married he said to her, "Now we will be our own family." And they were—they were for each other what they thought family should be. Right away between them it was a different matter from what either was accustomed to. She looked out for him; he looked out for her. Although they never spoke of it, she knew what they were doing: they were trying to set things right for each other. Before, he had been too much on his own, and she, too little. He had for years been lonely, badly in need of care and comfort. She had been beleaguered and no less in need. Marrying, they began at once to take care of each other. Many times over the years he had said to her, "What would I have done without you? Where would I be?" And these were not remarks made with a sarcastic intent. He was completely serious; he couldn't think of how his life would have gone without her. And hers, without him? He had *been* her life. If not for him, the whole course of things would have been different—it seemed to her that she herself would have come out differently. Who could say what would have been? What she knew for certain was only this: that she and Sol had set out together to make their own, to start everything new, and that in this they had succeeded. Whatever they had, they had because they themselves had created it; whatever was, was because they had made it so. Was this a small accomplishment? And as for what might have been—who could say? No one could say what might have been.

With a sigh she opened her eyes and looked out, beyond the television, through the window into the gray courtyard. There was nothing to see there. Across the way, from a wall of brick and windows, came music. Music? A terrible wailing—a rhythm like drums in a jungle. And yet the Russians listened to it from morning till night.

She felt very tired. Slowly she removed her glasses and set them on the table. With her fingertips she rubbed her eyes and then her cheeks. So gloomy, she thought. And she knew she did this to herself; she sat *thinking* herself into gloom. "So stop thinking," she muttered. "Too much is too much." For what was the point of thoughts like this? To remind herself that she was all alone in the world? But she wasn't, she had Rachel, she had someone to talk to.

But it was not the same. Naturally not. And it was not for talking that she had needed Sol. For talking they had been too busy, until it was too late; then they had the time but they didn't have the habit. No, it was his company she missed, his presence—it was his love. How he had loved her! It had been like an anchor, the great force of his need for her: for more than seventy years she had been held by it, secured. What was to keep her safe now?

She shivered. And what kind of thoughts were these? she wondered. Was this a way to pass the time? Foolish! It would be much better to be doing something than to sit here anymore with such thoughts. With such thoughts you might begin to feel that doing nothing was just as well as doing something, that moving a finger or a foot was not worth the effort it cost.

So, Rivke? she thought. *Nu?*

So all right, she told herself—she would, she would do something. But it would have to be in a little while. Right now she was too tired, exhausted. What she needed to do was stay here by the steam and doze, take a rest. There was no danger of sleeping through what remained of the day. Soon enough someone would call and wake her. It was possible, even, that it would be a happy call—a call bringing good news—although the probability of this was not the best. It was almost always bad news her children brought her: news of someone sick, getting divorced, leaving school, losing a job, taking drugs. The bad news would come, whatever she did—she had only to wait. And if she chose, while she waited, to sleep, she could sleep. There was no need to keep watch any longer. She was alone now; there was no one to watch over. Was there anything, after all, left for her to do but wait? No—nothing. Anything she was going to do in her life she had already done. Her work was finished.

4

That night she dreamed of being in Myra's house—walking through the long hall upstairs, bare feet brushed by carpet. It was dark in the hall, and she was frightened: she had lost her way. Along here somewhere, she knew, was the guest room—her room—but she was unable to tell which room this was. All the doors she passed were closed, and she was certain that she would not have closed her own door behind her; and yet if there was a door which remained open, she couldn't find it. At this point in the dream it occurred to her that the hallway was miles long, endless: it was full of doors—hundreds, perhaps thousands of them. Who could be asleep behind so many doors? she wondered. A strong desire came to her then to knock on all of them. But when she stopped in front of one she discovered that she could not bring herself to raise her fist—she was afraid of disturbing whoever might be sleeping there.

That was all. It was not a nightmare, she knew nightmares; in them, terrible things happened, knives appeared gleaming two feet long, guns blew out black smoke and noise that shook her awake in time to hear herself scream, men she understood to be murderers chased her, beat her with sticks and clubs and became invisible at the instant she turned her eyes to them. Nightmares she had plenty of; this could not be called by that name. But she was badly shaken by the dream. It was a dream with the feel of a nightmare; she woke from it perspiring and trembling.

Sitting up, she dug out her glasses from between the back

64

and seat cushions of the couch, and put them on. They didn't
help her to see—there was nothing to see but blackness yet—
but they made her feel more sure of herself, they took away
a little the scared feeling. For a while she sat thinking things
over in the dark. Then, because she knew she would not be
able to sleep now, she began inch by inch to work her legs
around until they slid off the couch and her heels bumped the
floor. Bearing down with her fists into the cushion on either
side of her, she rocked herself first forward and then up, and
for an instant she stilled her breath as she waited to see if her
legs would hold her. They did—they were not so bad today,
they were steady and ached only a little. Her neck and shoulders, however, were even worse this morning than usual. This
stiffness, with which she now woke daily (a new pain, as if she
needed one, on top of everything else—legs, heart, sugar, the
pressure of the blood), was the result of sleeping on the couch:
she spent her nights like an unwelcome guest for whom room
has been made grudgingly for only one night or two. Night
after night she lay stiffly on her side, her face pressed to the
back cushion, or on her back—like someone dead, eyes open
to the dark ceiling—and cramp in the neck or no, she kept
still until morning; this was necessary in order to avoid the
possibility of falling in the night. How could one rest comfort-
ably in this way? The answer of course was that it could not
be done. But she could not sleep alone in the bedroom; she
had tried this once—once was enough for her to understand
that without Sol beside her in the bed she would not be able
to sleep for even an hour—and after this, the first night she
had passed in her own home following the period of sitting
shivah at Myra's, she had begun the practice of nightly carrying blanket, sheet, and pillows into the living room. In the beginning she had opened up the couch for sleeping—for it was
in fact convertible into a bed (and in fact it was in this bed
that she and Sol had for some years slept, while the children
slept all together in the bedroom—but this was long ago al-

ready, this was forty, fifty years ago). The mattress concealed within the couch was not bad; naturally it was not as comfortable as the feather bed she and Sol had bought themselves for their fiftieth anniversary (also long ago! A quarter of a century had passed since then. Where had a quarter of a century gone?), but it was at least a mattress, it was wide enough so that one was free to turn from side to side or from front to back without danger of falling to the floor. With this arrangement only one problem remained, but this was by then a serious problem: she could not sleep. *Again* she could not sleep. She could not relax herself. Every night she lay still, listening and waiting, holding her breath lest the sound of it cover other, more important sounds, sounds that might serve as warnings. What exactly she was listening for—what exactly she was waiting for—she could not say. But all night she was awake listening. It was in the daytime, sitting at the kitchen table, that she slept; often she slept at the table for hours. Weeks passed in this way: her days lost to her in sleep, her nights full of nothing but waiting—waiting and a terrible anxiety. One morning, telling Myra about her night of no sleep, she remarked that she was contemplating spending her nights in the kitchen and her days in the bed—"Maybe then I could straighten myself out," she said. This was a joke; but that night as she lay awake again she asked herself if there might be something to it. Not that she was prepared to sit all night at the table. But if when the time came for sleeping she were to lie on the couch *without* opening it, could she perhaps, she wondered, fool herself into imagining it was still daytime—safe to sleep?

As it turned out, she could not fool herself (that was not, after all, so easy to do) but still this amounted to a much better arrangement—less comfortable, certainly, but better for her mind. She was not so anxious now; she was calmer because she felt that she was not *in bed*—she was resting only. She made up the couch each night: draped a folded sheet over the seat cushions, tucked it in lightly all around, pulled a blanket over her, and that was that. This way, it seemed to her, if an emergency were to arise, she was better prepared to get up in a hurry. She was not so helpless, this way; she was *ready*.

Ah, ready! she mocked herself as she stood on one foot, feeling with the toes of her other foot for her slippers. If God forbid it should ever become necessary to get moving at a moment's notice (*In the case of a fire? Was that it? A fire? A burglary? An intruder at the door?*), how quickly was it possible for her to move? She shook her head. *Foolish. Ready!* And once she had been a sensible person.

Muttering to herself (*idiocy! feeblemindedness!*), she moved like a sleepwalker, her arms outstretched in the dark, through the living room and to the kitchen. There, as she ran the tap for a glass of water, she considered once again her dream.

Not a dream at all. The thought came to her suddenly. Of course it was not a dream: only a memory.

Well, and this—she sipped lukewarm water meditatively, leaning against the sink—was not so strange after all. The memory itself, of staying with Myra after the funeral, was more dream to her than recollected fact. For a time after Sol was gone she'd been unable to take anything in properly; everything had come to her quieted down and muddled, with all the pieces of events put together in odd, baffling ways, all mixed up and muffled, as in a dream. Even such a simple matter as the route from the guest room to the bathroom down the hall would not stick in her mind—the idea of *direction*, the idea of "next to," even, was confusing to her—it had no meaning. Each night she *had* lost her way and become afraid— knowing it was not rational, this fear, not rational and not reasonable, but knowing making no difference—that she would not find her room at all and would have to walk up and down the hallway for the remainder of the night, finally collapsing in exhaustion on the carpet, where she would be discovered the next morning sprawled out (*half-dead ashamed like an ani-*

mal) by Myra and Harry. And she *had* been afraid to knock on their door, to ask them where she was supposed to go. What would they think? An old lady's forgetfulness. "Mama is becoming senile." This she felt she could not bear.

Like a dream, yes. Like *tonight's* dream, exactly, a nightmare that was not a nightmare, a nightmare without screaming. Without any sound. This—silence—was something she thought she remembered. But could it be that she had—as it seemed to her now that she had—remained silent throughout? Was this possible? No, not possible. She was only confused, remembering. What she remembered was too terrible; it was not possible to be *un*confused.

She had begun to tremble—she had to set the water glass down beside the sink. Oh, this was not a good idea, to stand in the darkness in the middle of the night thinking. And of *this*—this was the worst thing to think about. Never had there been a worse time—never. Nor could there be. From the moment when she had stood beside Sol in Mlotek's, the appetizing store, waiting for young Mlotek whom she had known since his childhood—the young man the grandson of the original—to take their order, and Sol had grasped her arm and said, "Rivke, help me, I can't stand on my feet," and before she could turn to him, before she could *answer* him—before she had taken a breath—he had fallen, tumbled bending at his knees face forward to the floor; and until long after she had come home alone from Myra's, to settle in once again to her own apartment (*not wanting to come back and yet they had sent her back—and hadn't she pleaded? hadn't she told them how much she did not want to come back?*), it had been the most terrible time in her life. The most terrible, and it was hard to believe it had *been*—hard to believe she had lived through it; and everything that had happened during this time was all mixed up in a jumble: she could not be sure what she remembered, and what she had dreamed of or invented as she thought it over. Was she remembering it right, the week in the hospital that followed the stroke?—and was it after all a week? It could have been more than a week, or less—watching him lie in the bed bloated and gray as if he were full of water, his face and his fingers swollen so fat it seemed to her they were ready to burst, and his eyes—his eyes open, too open, staring but *not* staring not seeing—so unlike *his* eyes, they were like glass and held no meaning. ("Gone already," the children said, "gone in his brain, only his heart still beats.") Watching him dying, standing by *watching* as beat by beat he left her—oh, this she remembered. She could rely on this, the memory of the worst thing that had happened in her life. *And* the silence. She remembered. Hers, his.

"Mama, he was lucky"—this was what they said to her later. Later when he was gone. "He felt nothing. The stroke took him away at once. It was only his heart that continued." Oh, yes, this was no dream, his face swollen gray, his eyes gaping, his mouth not a mouth any longer but a hole in his stretched, misshapen face; the tubes of all kinds into him and out; the yellow-black bruised skin of his wrists and neck and arms; and the smell, that bleachy sweetness, of the room, of *him*, his skin, his breath a sick-sweet cloud escaping from the edges of his mouth-hole, from around the thick clear tube taped there. Yes. She remembered.

And then? The rest of it? *Afterwards.* What? What then? She tried now to recall; she stood by the sink gripping the edge of the counter. Thinking. But no. Nothing. No memories. Of the funeral she recalled nothing. Not one thing. Gone. *If ever it had been.* This she couldn't help wondering: without memory, she could be sure of nothing. And—then—what of the time she had spent on Long Island, with Myra? *The hallway, in the night. And not wanting to leave.* And what else? What else?

Suddenly Rivke felt that she could not endure being in the darkness for another minute. She reached for the switch to turn on the overhead light and she was startled by what she saw first: the clock—which read only a quarter past three.

"*Mazel tov*," she murmured. Last night she had managed to sleep till four o'clock. Each night she woke a little earlier, and once awake she could not go back to sleep—it was her thoughts that prevented her; her mind would not rest once it had begun its work—but she could not begin the day in the middle of the night, either.

"This is already ridiculous." She spoke to herself quietly, and the sound of her own voice was very soothing to her. "So if you can't sleep," she said—louder, but pleasantly, as if to an acquaintance who had asked for her advice—"you can at least lie still for a while, can't you?" It was important, she knew, to rest her body, to protect what strength she had remaining; she had to give herself time to recover from the work of dragging herself around all day.

Returning to the living room, she instructed herself to rest her mind as well. Take a break, Rivke—this was something Sol had often said, to tease her. But a break she did not know how to take. What did it mean—"a break"? Was she to stop thinking—stop thinking altogether for a time? Sol used to say, "The problem is that you are too serious about your thinking." But how else could she be? This was something she had never understood. "You are more serious than is *necessary*," he had told her.

No, this didn't make sense to her at all. What was necessary? "I am as serious as I need to be," she would tell him, and he would laugh, he would shake his head. Perhaps, she thought, it would be a blessing to be not so serious—not so worried—but it was simply not possible for her. She was what she was. She had never been able to "take a break." Nor could she now, she reflected as she moved slowly to sit on the couch, fussing with the blankets so that she could lift her legs—what an effort this was!—and turn herself so that her legs could share the couch with the rest of her: she had already begun once again to replay her dream in her mind and to compare it with her memory.

The hall, the dark—she saw herself night after night wandering frightened in a blackness so thick it felt to her as if she were walking on the bottom of the sea. *And the days*—this thought jumped into her mind without warning and was a surprise to her—*the days were no better. Worse.*

Worse, yes. They—her children, their children, her nieces and nephews; and strangers too, the children and grandchildren of her nieces and nephews—sat staring at her. Not a word was spoken, and everyone's eyes were on her. But this could not be true. Certainly she was not recalling what had actually occurred but—yet again—was instead remembering a dream-version of the truth. Still, the memory was powerful now: a ring of silent children, young and old both, surrounding her where she sat, also silent, looking only into her own lap, in which one hand tightly grasped the wrist of the other.

And how long had this gone on? Ten days? Two weeks? Perhaps it had been a month. How long had she stayed with Myra? She had no idea. It might have been two months—it could be that it was more than two months. She could, of course, ask Rachel. But as she thought of this she felt uneasy; it seemed to her that to ask this question would be difficult and painful, and that it would require more strength—or perhaps it was not strength, but will, or craftiness—than she felt she now had; for there was a reason (at once she was certain of this, although she could not have said why; nor could she explain to herself why she was so disturbed by the thought) that she and Rachel, who spoke together of everything, never spoke of this—the period following the funeral.

Rivke stirred and shifted, trying to find a position that would be at least a little bit more comfortable. She turned on her side, kicking at the blankets and grasping them with both hands, pulling them up to her nose. It was only now that she realized she had left her glasses on, but she hadn't the energy to remove them. And when had she last felt she had the energy to do anything? Before she had lost Sol? Yes, before.

71

What had remained of her energy had left her then; it was as if he had pulled away with him whatever it was in her that had kept her strong. Even as she had stood watching him slip from her—slip fom life—she had felt her own hold on things draining away. What was left after this was a terrible looseness, a kind of weak, limp, exhausted self that was not in any way like her old self; the old self was lost for good.

And she—what remained of her after this—was left to sit in Myra's great living room amidst those who had come to pay their *shivah* calls; and what she had *felt* then was that she was lost—unmoored. And wasn't this true for all of them? Not only for her, but also for her sons, her daughter. And Rachel, who after the funeral had come to stay at Myra's as well. . . .

She remembered something now—here was something she had not known she could remember: that it had been Rachel who had been the first to hear of Sol's death; that it had been she who had broken the news to her. Suddenly Rivke recalled this quite clearly: Rachel taking her arm in the hospital corridor outside the room in which Sol had lain, and drawing her into a cubicle from which a young doctor fled, looking ashamed; Rachel sitting her down in a metal chair, kneeling on the floor before the chair, holding her hand, telling her, "Mama. He's gone now, he's passed."

What next came into her mind as she lay on the couch in the dark, her forehead to the upholstered back cushion, were pictures Rivke had not known were within her memory. Here was Amos, accepting condolences in his sister's living room: Amos, a big man, and stout—by six inches and seventy-five pounds the biggest in the family—standing in such a way that he appeared very frail; as he listened, head bowed, to his cousins speak of their sorrow, he looked to Rivke as if he were on the verge of toppling over. Even his voice, normally soft enough, had become smaller, softer, and frailer—from where she sat Rivke could not hear a word he said. His brothers, for their part, had with grief raised their voices, so that from anywhere in the house one could hear them shouting. And how jittery they were! They were on their feet at all times, jangling the change in their pockets, clearing their throats with a certain seriousness and calling loudly to one another as they moved about from room to room—straining to act, Rivke thought, the way they imagined grown men should under such circumstances: solemn and busy, but also philosophical—reconciled. But they were not reconciled; they were stunned and filled with despair—this was plain to her as she observed them in her memory. Reuben in particular seemed stricken. He drank too much—he drank constantly—roaming through Myra's house wearing an expression of bewilderment, a glass in hand always. His barking laugh emerged as a cough, an unhappy reflex, and even this sound had an edge of puzzlement to it; it rose at its end like a question.

It struck her now, as if she had never considered it before—and perhaps she hadn't, she thought; she had been occupied fully with her own grief—how hard they all had taken Sol's death. None of them had been prepared for it—it was a great shock; it had left them all severely shaken. But surely this was natural, for who could prepare for something like this? She could not have expected her children to be unshaken. Still, where Myra was concerned (slowly an image of her daughter in the days following the funeral gathered itself in Rivke's mind)—where Myra was concerned, wasn't there something more going on? Something *more* wrong?

Yes. Something—many things—wrong. Bit by bit came the picture: Myra shivering in a corner of the living room, complaining—though it was late May and the weather was good—that she was cold, so cold, and asking wouldn't someone *please for God's sake* shut the windows? Myra's hair was loose and had not been brushed; she had not applied lipstick or eye makeup or taken the trouble to dress in a presentable way. In her wrinkled blouse and dirty slacks—they must have been the ones she wore when she was at work in her garden; they were torn as well as muddy—she looked unlike herself: she, whose hair was always just so, coiled and pinned around her head, who dressed beautifully in such expensive clothes Rivke had ceased to ask their price, the numbers so astounded and disturbed her. And when before this had she last been seen barefaced? Twenty years? Rivke herself hardly recalled what her daughter, grown up, looked like without makeup.

Her eyes open in the darkness, she saw Myra—saw her as she had been *then*. Pale and jumpy, more jumpy still than any of her brothers, she started like a little animal when anyone came near her, then retreated, big-eyed, arms folded across her chest, to another corner of the room. Just like Amos, when she spoke it came out in a whisper—although this, the whispering, was not so strange as what she said: she said senseless, disconnected things. And as she spoke her arms unwound, unhugged her chest; her hands rose up and fluttered like small birds about her face. *So nervous!* Rivke thought. *Scared to death.* But not just scared—and not just afflicted by grief, or shock. Something else too.

This, the *something else*, was difficult—impossible—to understand. Rivke tried; she concentrated—and as she did she felt that she was *there* again, that the not-quite two years that had transpired since then had been erased, that she was once again in Myra's living room—but even so she could not grasp it, she could not find the *something else*.

She could see her daughter but could not make sense of what she saw—she could not get hold of it and name it, she could not say to herself what might be wrong with her.

And yet she *saw* her: she saw her standing still at first, and then in nervous action, rustling around the living room's perimeter, as inconstant and as fitful in her movements as a bit of paper flying in the wind. In close circular pursuit were relatives and friends who tried to offer up their sympathy; as soon as they were near enough to speak Myra would alter her path yet again, with a frightened glance backwards and a small, wild flapping of her hands. It was at this point (Rivke suddenly saw this, and the vision was another surprise) that Rachel would step in and take over, steering the perplexed niece or cousin away from her mother, who wanted only—this much was evident—to be left alone.

And was it true, as it now occurred to Rivke—the idea excited her strangely—that Rachel had done everything possible to arrange things thus? That she, Rachel, had in fact taken care of everything herself?

Rivke was so stirred by this thought she almost sat up; she had to force herself to be still, and instead of sitting she drew the blankets higher, pulled them over her head and pressed her nose to the scratchy familiar wool. Oh, yes, a memory was materializing which she felt to be a true, important memory: that everything had been left to Rachel. The job of greeting *shivah* callers and putting out glasses and plates and arranging the circle of liquor and soda bottles; the politely grateful acceptance of the traditional gifts of sweets, the cakes and cookies and baskets of fruit, and their distribution about the room; the cooking of breakfast for her father and for Rivke each morning, and the preparing of sandwiches as necessary for supper each night after the last of the visitors had gone—all of this was Rachel's to do. And how was it, thought Rivke, that she had not understood this at the time? She had not been able to see what was what, she thought, though it was perfectly obvious to her now that something had been up. There was not only Myra's extraordinary appearance and behavior to consider; there was the way they—Rachel and her brother Mark—had packed *her* up and bustled her out of Myra's house, so abruptly, so early in the morning.

This she remembered.

Rachel had cried. She cried, while at the same time saying, "Grandma, I have to take you home now. I'm sorry." Rivke was dumbfounded. She sat on the bed looking at her granddaughter for a long time. She didn't speak at first because she had nothing to say and had not made out exactly what the meaning of Rachel's words was. She had not yet given any serious thought to what her life would be like without her husband, and it had never entered her mind that she might live alone—she had never in her life been alone.

Finally, she said the only thing she could think of. "Home?" she said. "To Brighton? Now?" For certainly, she thought in her confusion, she had misunderstood Rachel's word "home"; certainly she would not be sent back to the apartment in which she had lived for so many years with Sol?

"Yes, now," Rachel said. "Today. I'm sorry." And she continued to cry.

Like children running away while their parents slept—no, Rivke thought: like criminals fleeing after doing their work of harm, she and Rachel worked quickly in guilty, anxious silence, getting her washed and dressed, folding her clothes and tucking them into her suitcase. Soon they were climbing into Mark's car, which she only then discovered had been waiting in front of the house. How early it must have been when they had summoned him!—for it was not yet six o'clock when the three of them, Rivke and her daughter's two children, began the trip back to Brooklyn.

Like criminals! Speeding her home, with no good-byes, without a word to her daughter.

"She's not feeling well, Grandma." This was Mark, speaking to her without turning to face her as he drove. He spoke in such a tone that one would use to converse with a stranger. "She's not feeling well," he repeated. "She feels she needs to be by herself now. But you'll be able to talk to her on the phone in a day or two."

A lie. It was weeks before she heard from Myra by telephone, and the conversation at that time was a brief, stiff exchange of greetings that left Rivke feeling frightened. Rachel assured her that she need not be upset or worried, and Rivke understood that it was fraudulent—this behaving as if nothing out of the ordinary were going on—but she could not think what she might *do* about it, and she could not determine the significance of the fraud. What was going on? What did it mean? Alone in her apartment, where she had not expected to be, she could do nothing—neither eat nor sleep, nor think clearly. She knew that something very bad had happened—was happening—concerning her daughter; but no one would speak the truth about it to her. No one would speak about it at all.

Rivke, lying on her side, covered from head to toe by her blankets, considered the strangeness of this. No one would speak—and now almost two years had passed and still not a word had been spoken about it. But she was not stupid (she told herself wryly): she knew—and why did they act as if she did not?—about the last time Myra had been "not well," the last time she had looked and behaved as she had after her father's death. She remembered—how could she forget? She had been forbidden for months to see her. Refused access to her own daughter! Ah, for this she would never forgive Harry Lieber. "I'm sorry, Mom"—this was what her daughter's husband had told her nearly thirty years ago—"but Myra's not well, she's very depressed. This is a bad time for her, it's better if you stay away for a while."

And yet whose fault was this depression?

"Your father's fault," Rivke had said plainly to Rachel when her granddaughter had asked her, years ago now, when she was still in high school, what had been responsible for that "bad time" her mother had had. "The fault of her husband. She never had such a problem before she married your father." And then Rachel had astonished Rivke with her next question: "Don't you think it's more likely that it was me?"

"How you? You were a baby."

"My birth, I mean," Rachel said. "*Having* a baby."

"Oh, this is nonsense, *mamaleh*," Rivke told her. "It was your father. About this I'm certain. Yelling, always yelling. He would scare her out of her wits. She had a very delicate nature, your mother. She still has. She never liked so much yelling."

"Maybe not. Who likes yelling? But that doesn't seem a real terrific reason, does it, for taking to your bed for eight years?"

"Is this sarcastic?" Rivke said. At sixteen, seventeen, the child had been sometimes very difficult to talk to. "Because this is not a subject for your sarcasm. Besides, she was out of bed plenty. You remember only the worst."

But she too remembered the worst—what for her, at any rate, had been the worst: that period of several months when she had not been allowed to see or speak to Myra at all. "It's necessary," her son-in-law had said. Necessary! What did he know about necessary? A mother's place was with her daughter when the daughter was in trouble. Before this, Harry had *come* to her for help. Who but Rivke could Harry turn to? Who else could he trust? Then suddenly she was banished from the house, she was deprived even of the child, her daughter's daughter—the child who was practically her own, she had spent so much time with her almost from the moment of her birth. For Myra *was* often not quite well, it was true; she was often in bed or out making visits to the doctor, and always it was Rivke who took over the care of the child then.

Rachel remembered this better than one would expect. She had once told Rivke that she recalled an afternoon when she had returned from kindergarten eager to show her mother something she had made, but Rivke, who had picked her up after school, as often she did, had taken her to her own apartment instead of to Myra and Harry's, a few blocks away. This too was a common occurrence, and usually the child didn't mind, for Rivke's home was as much home to her as was the other. But on this day, she had objected strenuously. "I threw a terrible fit, didn't I! I was *furious* at you."

Rivke remembered this also. "Oh, yes, you cried, 'I want my mother, give me my mother, I don't want *you*, I hate *you*.'

But I couldn't let you bother her, she was home sleeping. She had just come back from her doctor and she was worn out."

"She was *always* worn out," Rachel said. "She was worn out till I was eight years old."

"She was sick, *mamaleh*," Rivke said gently. "Sick" was the word Harry had used, that day when he'd told her she could not see her daughter "for a while." It was Harry's word, not hers, but sometimes she found herself using it, for "sick" made the whole mysterious business sound not so unreasonable. It made good sense to stay in bed if one were sick. And in any case it was untrue that Myra had been in bed *all* of the time. She had had her good periods—sometimes lasting for weeks and into months. During these periods everyone would count: two weeks, three weeks, four, six, seven—and believe hopefully that this time she would stay well. Rivke herself half expected, when she was finally invited to return to the Lieber household—invited to return as if nothing had happened!—that Myra *would* at last be altogether well. This was not the case; but she was, however, pregnant with Mark—and what seemed to be was that Harry needed Rivke's help badly enough to overlook everything else—whatever "everything else" was, for he had never troubled to make it clear to Rivke why she had been turned away to begin with.

No, she would never forgive Harry for that time—never. And it dawned on her now that she had been living for years in dread of a recurrence of this, of her banishment. She had never let herself think of it, but it had been inside her, a secret fear, all those years—and then there it was once again. After so long, it happened—and this time she was sent away to live out the rest of her life alone. This was unnatural, it was crazy. She knew that for it to have been allowed Myra must have been in very bad shape, worse perhaps—probably—than the time before. But what did she not know was whether, while her grandchildren were carrying her so hurriedly back to Brooklyn, Myra had been taken to a hospital to be treated for her grief. This was what, taking everything into account, Rivke now believed.

But she would never *know.* Who could she ask? She could not ask Myra; to Myra she did not even speak of that bad time of decades earlier. And she could not ask Rachel. She could not say why—but she felt it strongly; she was sure that asking her would be wrong.

And yet: was it right that she, at the age of eighty-seven, had been sent to an empty apartment to live out what remained of her life by herself? For this too she held Myra's husband responsible. "Your father wants his wife to himself," Rivke often told Rachel. And she would add, slyly, "And why not? Who can blame him? It's natural, no? Who wants to have an old lady around?" Rachel did not answer. On this and on all other matters relating to her father she was mute. All right, then: let her be mute. But Rivke understood how it was between a husband and a wife on the subject of a mother coming into their home to live. Hadn't she and Sol argued over *her* mother? Of course, *she* had not wanted her mother with them any more than he had, so their argument had been especially complex and confusing. In fact (this she recalled with a sharp pull of breath—at times he had been so self-righteous!), Sol had been more willing than she to take Mina in. "Yes," he had said in the end, "it is true that to get along with her is very difficult, and it is true that she is a hard woman, and it is also true that I don't like her. But she is so old and there is no one else now. We have no choice, Rivke."

Old! She had to laugh. Her mother had been sixty-seven at the time of her death, two months after she and Sol had taken her. They were the last ones. When in 1925 her parents had first come to the United States, they had stayed with Leah. This did not work out. Mina and her eldest daughter fought day and night for months, and Mina finally declared that she could not live any longer with Leah; she would, she said, move in with Essie. Rivke, next in age to Leah, could have been insulted, but her relations with Mina had always been so strained she was only relieved. This second arrangement, though, did not last long either. It was, if anything, a worse mistake. Mina and Essie's husband, Zalmen, argued with much bitterness over everything; Essie fluttered between them anxiously, trying in vain to make peace, while Papa, who had been unhappy in the first place about coming to America, grew more and more silent and gloomy. Then, not three months after Mina and Shmuel had moved in with Essie, Shmuel had a heart attack and died instantly—quietly; as he had lived—in his sleep. After this, Mina became harder still. She was unable to get along with anyone: she was cold to Essie, who had once been her favorite, and colder yet to Essie's only child, Meyer; with Essie's husband she could not manage even a moment of civil conversation (it had to be acknowledged that nobody could get along with Zalmen—he was a cruel and stupid man, and when he died young there was no one willing to mourn him but Essie; even his own son despised him—but Mina was stubborn and would not avoid or ignore him as others in the family did; she set herself directly in his path, deliberately provoking him, and Essie feared for her life: she was truly afraid her husband would kill her mother).

The children had a conference. In less than a year, Mina had gone through two of them; a plan had to be worked out. Of Mina's eight children, six were in the United States—no one was left in the old country: Reuven, the youngest son, had died the year after Rivke had left home; the youngest daughter, Sheine, was in Argentina, where as it turned out she would remain for life. There were four children, thus, who remained candidates for housing their mother: Heschel, the eldest, a dressmaker; Shlomo, who was in this country called Moe, and who at that time was still fooling with this and that but later came to open his own grocery; Yischak, called Izzy, who in 1926 was still in the millinery trade along with Sol; and Rivke, the only remaining daughter in America. Shlomo and Yischak were in agreement that Rivke should take Mina next, but Heschel, the wisest of all of them, understood that this would be the worst arrangement possible, and he volunteered to take her himself. This was a noble offer, as his wife had her hands full already with nine children, two still infants, and it shamed Rivke; it did not, however, shame her enough to protest.

Mina lived with Heschel's family for almost five years. It was never clear exactly what happened at the end of that time between her and her daughter-in-law, but the result was that Heschel spoke privately to Moe—who by now had his own store in Williamsburg—and asked him to take over. So then it was Moe for a couple of months, and then the youngest living son, Izzy, took his turn (again this was arranged quietly, between the brothers; Izzy was now working for Moe in the grocery). Finally, in January—it was 1932—just after Rivke discovered she was pregnant again (for the last time, as it turned out), Mina came to her. But not before Rivke and Sol argued, pointlessly and at great length, about it. Rivke for weeks could not admit to herself that there was no alternative plan available; but in the end there was nothing to do but accept it—there was no way out: Mina had exhausted all other possibilities.

The two months that Mina was with Rivke she complained without pause: nothing was good enough for her. She interfered with Rivke's raising of her sons, criticizing her before them—humiliating her. Rivke would try to talk to her and she would find herself fumbling for words, Mina so discomfited her—she would stare at her, no expression whatsoever on her stern face. One could not get through to her. At night Rivke wept, quietly so Mina on her cot in the foyer would not hear. Mina of course did hear. How could she fail to? The apartment was overcrowded; the situation was hopeless, unmanageable. Amos was already in his second year at Brooklyn College— he had entered at sixteen, brilliant as well as big for his age— and he was desperate for some quiet, some privacy. This was not possible. All four boys slept in the bedroom, and five-year-old Sammy could not be trusted to keep his hands off anything; he was always into Amos's books and notes. Rivke and

Sol, sleeping in the living room, whispered and worried. The apartment seemed in danger of bursting with its burden of people and tension.

Mina's death, in March, of a massive stroke, was a great shock to Rivke. Still, it was easier to mourn her mother than it had been to talk to her. She had never felt an hour's ease with her—this Rivke allowed herself to admit only after Mina's death, and then only silently. To whom would she have spoken of such things? Early in their marriage she had hinted to Sol that between Mina and her all was not as it should be, that even—even? especially!—as a child she had not felt for her what she wished to feel. But when he did not ask ("How then did you feel?"), she closed her mouth; she had said enough. What she felt was a secret she had guarded all of her life. To her brothers and sisters, whom she might have confided in, she could not bring herself to speak; there was in her mind the uneasy question of whether the lack was in *her*—not in Mina. What did the others feel for her? She would never know now, of course; all but Sheine, the baby of the family, were gone, and Sheine Rivke had not seen for twenty-five years, since her second (and surely last) visit to the States. And to her father? She would not have dared to speak to him of her mother. She loved him dearly; she could not bear the thought of distressing him with unhappy revelations. How he himself had felt about Mina Rivke could not guess. Who could tell? He must have loved her, she thought: why else would he have married her? She was not so young when they married—not for those times—she was twenty-four; nor was she beautiful or rich.

Mina was Shmuel's second wife, a good friend to the first, who had died young, childless. Of her father's first marriage Rivke knew nothing more than this. Neither Mina nor Shmuel had ever spoken of it; she had learned of its existence only because a gossipy aunt, her father's younger sister, had said too much one afternoon to ten-year-old Rivke. It was from this same aunt that Rivke had learned her mother's age at the time of her marriage (her mother would never speak of matters of this type, she said they were no business of her children) and that Mina's parents had very nearly given up hope by that time. They had been grateful, Tante Iteleh told Rivke, when Shmuel Gebiner offered to marry their daughter.

Even now, close to sixty years after his death, Rivke smiled tenderly thinking of her father, remembering him brought forth such affectionate feelings. How she had worshiped him in her childhood! From the couch where she lay she called up the image of him at work: he had been a barrel-maker; she had loved to watch him bend the narrow strips of wood, forcing them into the necessary arc and binding them with the hoops with which he sometimes let her play. While he cut and worked the staves, she sat contentedly on a barrel he had made. She would be very still, silently taking in the sight of her papa concentrating so hard on his labor and the scent of the wood which filled her nostrils in a way that dizzied her. The wood smell was everywhere—Papa himself smelled of damp wood, and at night when he stroked her hair in his absent way, before she went to sleep, she would place her head on his chest and take deep breaths of him.

There was not much talk between them: he was a quiet man, not given to speech as often as to gesture, with a soft voice for her when he chose to use it, and soft, kind-looking features. A kind man, altogether. His eyes often had a moist look that made her worry, but she never did see him cry until he came to America—then she saw him cry many times. She would sit with him in Leah's, then Essie's, kitchen, holding his hand, and from under the ragged droop of his whitish eyebrows he would watch her with his wet eyes—blue that matched hers. She watched him in return; his free hand crept every so often into his beard and pulled at it—his tendrily pale yellow beard which dangled to the middle of his chest. There was nothing to say so she said nothing; she was helpless in the face of his sorrow. Once in a while as they sat he would smile at her—faintly, but still it was a smile—and press her hand a little bit tighter. This made her happy. Even in her childhood he had not often smiled—he seemed at most times to be too tired to smile—but when he did Rivke felt it as a triumph of her own.

Mina, now, on the other hand, never smiled; in her case it appeared to be a matter of principle. Her mouth held an expression that was a straight line, neither frown nor smile. She was stone cold, a statue—and always there seemed to have been a special coldness in her toward Rivke, for reasons Rivke could not identify. She was a middle child: she had sisters both older and younger as well as brothers. Why had she been singled out for particular hardness toward her? If in fact it was hardness, if it was not bitterness, anger, resentment—if it was anything at all. It was of course possible that Mina had been equally cold in her feeling toward all her children, that she had not had anything in particular against Rivke from the beginning, but that only Rivke had taken her indifference to heart this way, and that Rivke's wistfulness had turned Mina against her. It was possible that Mina could not forgive her daughter for willing her to be some way other than the only way she was able to be. Still and all—whatever the explanation—there was bad feeling between mother and daughter from start to finish, and Rivke as a girl had been unable to prevent herself from trying to alter this: she made efforts again and again to please her mother—or, if she could not manage that—and she could not—to obtain her full attention for a moment or two. This also could not be done.

Even after she had left childhood and Europe both far behind, Rivke made an effort to win over her mother. One final effort, she thought at the time (though this turned out not to be the case; she would instead try and try again until her mother's death, and even after her death, even to this day—and *this* was crazy—she would sometimes catch herself thinking: Mama would be proud of *this*, *this* would please Mama).

For this "last" attempt to please her, Rivke planned to send back to Łomża an expensive gift—a fancy nightgown she had her eye on, very luxurious and beautiful. She was full of guilt when she thought of spending the money, however, for which Sol, her husband of only two years, had worked so hard; but she wanted very badly to do this, and when she told him, he shrugged and said he didn't mind. Either he understood, or else he didn't feel it was necessary for him to understand. But because he did not ask for an explanation, Rivke fretted in secret. She told herself she could not justify the expense, they could not afford to buy fancy gifts no matter for whom. Also— she continued the argument with herself—Mina had done nothing to deserve a gift and furthermore was likely to be unappreciative. Then she reminded herself that it was uncertain whether or not her parents would ever make their way to the United States, and that she thus did not know if she would ever in her life see them again. How could it hurt, she ended up wondering, to send a lovely gift to her mother?

But it did hurt, a year later, when her sister Essie came over from Poland, alone, as Rivke had done five years earlier, and spoke of the nightgown, mentioning casually that Mina had given it to *her* as soon as the package from America arrived. "It didn't fit Mama?" Rivke asked, her heart pounding in her ears. "No," Essie said. "It fit. But she said I should have it." She spoke very matter-of-factly, as if this were of no consequence. Rivke immediately changed the subject—she would not give her younger sister the satisfaction of seeing how badly hurt she was. And, still later, after Mina and Shmuel themselves came—this was already a dozen years after the nightgown had been sent—when Rivke summoned up the courage to ask her mother why she had given away her gift, Mina said, "What did I need such a thing for?" and laughed her abrupt hoarse laugh, in which no amusement was present. It was then that Rivke told herself to give up forever expecting anything from her mother. Mina had no normal, motherly feelings, she told herself—not, in any case, for her. Yet even so it was hard to relinquish such an old habit, this habit of need and desire. But at least, from that time on, she began at once to scold herself as soon as the thought—"Maybe *this* will make Mama happy"—crossed her mind. And indeed the thought did come to her with less frequency after Shmuel's death, for with her father gone it was easier to give up the old claims to her mother's affection; it had been he, after all, not she, whom Rivke loved: there was nothing any longer to cause her to think she *ought* to love Mina, even if she was obliged to behave as if she did—as a daughter should—for the sake of appearances, and also because it was only right.

She had never uttered the words *I hate her* to a living soul (though it was possible her brother Heschel had surmised them) until the day she spoke them to her granddaughter and shocked both Rachel and herself—one of many things she heard herself saying to Rachel that surprised her, things she had supposed she'd never say to anyone. After this confession Rivke drew in a long breath and waited for her granddaughter's reaction. But Rachel, after a brief silence, did not say what Rivke feared most to hear—"This is wrong, you must not feel this," or "You are mistaken, you *do not* feel this"—but instead groaned and murmured, "Oh, Grandma, how *awful*. You poor thing."

And what a relief this was, to receive this sympathy! What a relief simply to say what was on her mind after so many years of keeping to herself everything that was important to her. And while it was remarkable enough, she thought, that she had found a confidante that could be trusted in her granddaughter, more remarkable still was that the last person in whom she had confided this way had been her *own* grandmother—Mina's mother, Ruchel, for whom Rachel had been named. This was going back a great many years. But, oh, as a child, a small child, Rivke had adored her so! To this day she felt devoted to her. Never mind that Ruchel was already elderly at the time of Rivke's birth—she could not have loved her granddaughter more, or been kinder to her, if she had been young; perhaps she would have loved her less. And although she lived for only nine more years, it was long enough for a lifetime bond—a bond to last for all of Rivke's life—to form. She had always planned to name her own daughter for Ruchel, but Mina's death, coming as it had while Rivke still carried the child, made her feel obliged to name the baby after her; for she could not tolerate the thought of what the others would say, or worse yet think, if she did not do so. But at Myra's birth she made up her mind that *her* daughter, her daughter's daughter, would be named for Ruchel.

What a wonderful woman she had been! She had been a marvel of a woman—a jewel. Loving, patient, full of fun, she was always ready with a story or a joke for her granddaughter. And yet between her and her only daughter there had been no sweetness—nothing, no tenderness. Between them Rivke could see no connection. Mina would look on without speaking when Rivke ran from the house on her grandmother's heels. Hanging on to Ruchel's skirts, she would follow her through the streets—she had a little business, peddling the rolls and cakes she made. When they stopped to sit, Rivke would climb into her grandmother's lap and beg for stories and songs. Also she would tell her secrets—all of her most treasured child-secrets (except the most dreadful one: her feelings for her mother; even at this age she knew she could not speak of that to Ruchel, no matter how far apart mother and daughter were). Ruchel would sit, her skirts spread all around her, and make jokes with her customers as she sold her baked goods; in between sales she would talk or sing to her granddaughter, she would listen gravely as small Rivke whispered into her ear all her private business. To no one but Ruchel could Rivke speak her mind. Was it not an amazing thing that eight decades later she would be telling her secrets to a second Ruchel?

How strange life was! To have two confidantes in a lifetime:

grandmother, granddaughter—this was something truly extraordinary. A piece of good fortune. And with a thought like this, which was not only interesting but filled her with gladness, Rivke had no patience to lie still anymore. She peered out from the blankets and was relieved to find that daylight was beginning its slow passage into the room, stirring up the dust and lighting all the empty corners and bare walls. At last, morning. Thoughts of the two Ruchels, of her mother, her father, her youth, her life as it used to be, fled from her mind immediately. She could begin the day now: get herself up from the couch, wash her face, insert her teeth, boil a kettleful of water, fix a little breakfast. Another day—and it would be gone before she knew it, lost in her dreaming, if she did not take hold of it. Best to begin along with the sun: as it rose, so too would she. Not nearly so grandly, of course, she thought with a little shrug and a smile to herself as she gathered her strength for the task, but—without question—every bit as slowly.

5

"Myraleh, tell me please, what day is today?"

"Today is Friday, Mama."

"Friday." This was a surprise. "And how is it Friday already?"

"*How* is it Friday, Mama? Like always."

"But so fast," Rivke said. "I don't know where the week goes. The days run away."

"Time flies," Myra agreed.

"But if it's Friday already"—Rivke spoke mainly to herself, muttering—"I have to then make *shabes*. This it's hard to believe I forgot."

"Oh, Ma," Myra said, "why don't you just skip it for once?"

"Skip *shabes*?" Rivke chuckled. "I don't think this is possible. Once a week comes *shabes*. About this a person doesn't have a choice."

"What I *mean*"—Myra's impatience was plain—"is skip the preparation. It's too much for you, it tires you out."

"*Ach*," Rivke said. "Too much for me it isn't." This wasn't true. For some time she had felt that it really was too much for her. It was only for *shabes* that she cooked; the rest of the week she ate cold cereal, fruit, pot cheese, crackers. For supper she might boil an egg or heat canned soup; for lunch she nibbled lettuce leaves, or salted and ate a good tomato if she happened to have one—it was enough for her. But on Fridays she had to gather all her strength to cook a chicken, steam a potful of rice, make a *tsimes* if someone had remembered during the week to bring her sweet potatoes and carrots—a box of prunes she always had—and peel and chop vegetables for

90

soup. "*Shabes* is *shabes*," she told Myra. "For this I have no choice but to prepare."

"But if just once you *didn't* make *shabes*, would it be the end of the world?"

"The end of the world, no. But if somebody comes, there has to be to eat."

"If someone *comes*," Myra said—oh, she was irritated, Rivke could tell by the way she stretched out "comes" into two parts, as if she were singing: *cah-ums*—"somebody can go *down*"—*dow-un*, more singing—"and on Brighton Beach Avenue pick up a take-out chicken from Fechter's."

"Myra," Rivke said, "please. For what do I need a take-out chicken? I can take out of the freezer right now my own chicken to cook and you know yourself it will taste better than from Fechter's."

She expected to hear, "You're right, Mama," but Myra said, "*First* of all, a chicken's not going to defrost in time for you to cook it before *shabes*—you should have taken it out last night. And *second* of all, who are you expecting to come, anyway? Last week you were angry, you said a whole chicken and a pot of cabbage soup went to waste because no one came. 'I can't eat so much,' you told me. 'How can I eat so much?' If you don't cook so much, you won't waste so much."

"But tomorrow someone might come."

"*Who?*"

"Who? I don't know who. I have five children."

"I *know*, Ma, but . . ." But she stopped, and after a pause long enough to make Rivke wonder what she had planned to say, all that finally emerged was, "I just hate to see you tire yourself with cooking."

"Oh, tire, shmire," Rivke said and hoped for a laugh.

Myra instead sighed. "I'll tell you what, Ma. Why don't you do whatever you want to do."

"Ah, what I want to do! *This* would be nice, if I could do what I want to do. I'd go dancing, I'd take a trip someplace."

Still no laugh. "I'm joking, *mamaleh*," she said gently. "This was a joke, you understand. Where would I go for a trip?" Myra kept silent. Rivke, with a sigh of her own, said, "*Tokhter*, will you tell me something? If today is Friday, then what is the number—the date?"

"The fifteenth," Myra said, and added after a second, "of March."

"Of March I know," Rivke said. "By you, I don't know what month is this?" She was startled herself by how angry she sounded.

"Well, I'm sorry, Mama, but—"

"When comes the day that I can't tell you what is the month, this is when you'll know it's finished with me. All right?"

"Oh, Ma, listen—"

"It wouldn't hurt you, Myra—would it hurt you?—to say, 'All right, Mama'?"

"All right, Mama," said Myra.

Rivke took a moment to collect herself—she didn't like this, for such a feeling to come to her so quickly—and only when she was once again able to speak pleasantly did she say what she wanted to say. "So if it's already the fifteenth of March, then I'm thinking that *peysekh* is coming soon, yes?"

"Yes, that's right—in three weeks—and it's a good thing you reminded me because I needed to talk to you about that. Last night Rachel called to ask me what we're doing this year for the holiday."

"Yes? And what did you say?"

"That's what I wanted to talk about. She asked me if I'd make a seder—well, not really a seder, but a big dinner, like a turkey dinner maybe, you know, like you used to do when she and Mark were too little to sit still for a seder? But I don't know, it seems like such a lot of work for just the four of us— because it would be only you and me and Harry and Rachel; Mark I think is planning to go to the first-night seder at his in-laws'. So I just don't know. What do you think?"

"It's Papa's birthday, *peysekh*."

"I *know* that, Ma. Rachel knows too, that's why she was concerned. Naturally we don't want you to be alone for this. That's the reason I'm asking you what you want to do. We'll do something, this much I promise. I'm just not sure what, exactly. But I don't want you to worry about it."

"Worried I'm not," Rivke said. "What happens will happen. To tell you the truth, where I was last year for *peysekh* I don't even remember."

"Last year you were with Amos and Frances. You don't remember? You spent the whole week with them."

"Oh, yes, I remember now." In fact she didn't—she had no memory of this at all—but she could see that today was not a good day to tell Myra something like this; she would leap on it right away as evidence of her feebleness. Besides, Rivke told herself, it was likely that if she thought about it later, when she could concentrate, the memory would come to her. In the meantime, before Myra could ask her any questions, she said, "You know, Myraleh, for a seder I don't have so much strength anymore—"

"Oh, Ma," Myra interrupted, "no one expects you to make a seder, for God's sake. You haven't made a seder for—for I don't know how long."

"I wasn't thinking I was going to make a seder," Rivke said mildly. "Old I am, crazy I'm not. I was only going to say that while a seder is one thing, Papa's birthday is something else."

"Ma—I told you. You won't be alone."

"Oh, alone." She pronounced the word with distaste. "I'm always alone."

"You're not always alone."

"Visits are visits," Rivke said, "and alone is alone. I feel alone."

To this Myra seemed to have nothing to say, and Rivke after a moment went on, "Do you know what I sometimes think? I sometimes think that if Papa had known what was in store for me, he wouldn't have left me."

"Oh, Ma. To have these kinds of—"

"Listen, Myraleh, I'm telling you something. Papa must have thought: She'll be all right; I can go. He left me so fast I didn't have time to tell him he was wrong. If there had been time to talk, I would have said, 'Sol, you're making a mistake.' But he should have known himself that this was a mistake."

"Mama," Myra said, "be reasonable."

"Reasonable." Rivke considered this. "What's reasonable? Is it to you reasonable that we're talking now about making a celebration of Papa's birthday without Papa?"

"Oh, no, Ma, this is up to you. If you'd rather *not* celebrate Papa's birthday, all you have to do is tell me."

"This is not the point," Rivke said.

"Tell me what's the point, then, Mama."

Rivke was silent, thinking. Why should it be, she wondered, that what was obvious to her was never obvious to her children? There were some things that could not be *said*: things for which words were not enough—would never *be* enough, no matter how many words one strung together. One had to *know*.

For a little while she remained silent, listening to Myra's silence—an aggravated, quick-breathing silence—at the other end of the line. Finally she said, "Do you remember, Myra, the song, a *yidisheh* song, *Vos Geven iz Geven un Nishto?*"

"I don't think I ever knew it."

"*Vos geven iz geven un nishto,*" Rivke sang—not well; she had some difficulty remembering the melody. "What was, was, and isn't anymore," she translated. "This is what the song says."

"A sad song," Myra said. But it seemed to Rivke that she spoke reluctantly.

"That's right, it's a sad song. *Vos geven iz geven:* everything that once was is now gone."

"Ma—not everything is gone."

"Ah, this is true," Rivke said. "It's true: I'm still here. Old, but here. Right?" She coughed out a short laugh and didn't wait for a response. "But I'll tell you what, *mamaleh*. I'm here, and I'm also not here. Most of me is already gone, most of what I was. This is what happens. You'll see it yourself. The years go by; time takes away. Time takes away, and what does it give back?" Rivke paused; she laughed—but as she laughed it dawned on her suddenly that she was exhausted; she was so thoroughly tired she wasn't sure she could continue the conversation for even a minute longer. "It gives back nothing," she said. And then: "Myraleh, I think I need now to go lie down. We'll talk tomorrow in the morning."

"Mama, are you okay?"

"Okay, yes. Don't get scared. I just got tired all of a sudden. Now I'm going to take a nap, I think. Or maybe I'll go in the bath."

"A bath is a good idea, Ma, a bath is very restful. But promise me that if you take a bath you'll be careful getting in and out."

"Careful I am always."

Yes, a bath *was* a good idea, she thought as she hung up the phone. It was just what she needed; for she was not only tired, she also had a bad feeling in her that she could not explain and wanted to be rid of, and a nap couldn't be relied on for that—a nap might even sink the feeling deeper into her—while a good hot bath might float it away.

She had always like a bath. She would take a bath every day—twice a day, even—if it were only not so difficult for her to get out of the tub when she was through. Even so she managed it three, sometimes four times a week. She had devised, over the years, a method for getting herself out of the bath which—though it took forever—was safe and had never yet failed her. First she would grasp with her left hand the soap dish that was cemented into the wall over the tub, at the same time pushing with her right hand on the edge of the tub itself. Then, proceeding slowly and resting often, she would bring herself up into a crouch (much patience was required for this, for sometimes the process took twenty minutes or more: she would reach the necessary position and her ankles would tremble so that she would have to drop forward in the tub to her knees, remain there for a moment to collect her strength, then try again, pushing backwards until she was on her feet once more—and then her ankles would again give way and she would return to her knees, pause again for a rest, rock back to her feet, and so on—over and over again). When finally she was planted firmly on the balls of her feet, the next step was to turn herself around (as she did this she imagined that she looked like a great pink frog) to face, squatting, the back of the tub. Then came the hardest part. With first her left hand and then her right she had to reach for the towel bar above the toilet, which stood just beside the tub. To manage this took at least a dozen attempts. But once she had grabbed hold of it, she could use the towel bar to pull herself up until she was half-standing; and from there it wasn't so difficult—one hand pulling on the towel bar, the other pushing on the toilet—to stand up altogether. All that was needed now was to keep hold of the towel bar and concentrate on balancing on one leg as she raised the other over the side of the tub—then she was finished.

It was a pity, she thought, that no one would ever see how well she could accomplish such a trick at her age. The only person who had ever seen her do this, of course, was Sol. For a long time *he* had hoisted her up and out of the tub when she was through with her bath, but when he began to grow too weak and unsteady himself, she had had to work out her own system. He used to come in to watch—he came running when he heard the water gurgling as it started to drain from the tub—and though she wouldn't let him help (that would be the end of both of them, she thought, if he fell down while tugging on her), she didn't mind if he watched from the doorway. He kept quiet, watching with his arms folded and his expression serious—he knew enough not to distract her with talk until she was safely out of the tub—and when she was out, and stood dripping in the center of the bathroom trying to catch her breath and waiting for her heart to slow down, he would shake his head and murmur, "Acrobat."

She was already in the bathroom and had begun to draw her bath when she remembered the chicken she had meant to thaw. Returning to the kitchen, she told herself—repeating it out loud several times—that she mustn't forget the water running in the bathtub. One afternoon not long ago she had started a bath and when the telephone rang forgot about it; the Russian lady downstairs had come up screaming in her Cossack language—Rivke had been badly frightened by her—and it was not until the woman, still scolding and carrying on, had pushed past her and run into the bathroom to shut off the water herself that Rivke understood that she had flooded the bathroom below hers.

In the kitchen she stuck her head in the freezer and surveyed what was there: two chickens left of the four that Myra had bought the last time she'd shopped for her. She looked from one to the other and finally took the smaller one from the freezer and set it on the countertop to thaw. Maybe it would, she thought, and maybe it wouldn't. If it didn't, she could always hold it under hot water to finish the job. She calculated how much time it would take to cut it in pieces and boil it; then she opened the broom closet and looked behind the door at the calendar she kept tacked up there—she had to look for a long time before she could read the small print—to see what time she was supposed to *bentsh* candles tonight. Another rapid calculation, and she determined that if the chicken was still icy at four o'clock she would try, with a little hot water, to help it along.

Oh, but what a difference from how preparing for *shabes* used to be. She would be cooking from six o'clock in the morning—not just a boiled chicken and a soup with carrots and onions and celery, plain rice, the simplest *tsimes*; but roast chicken and soup with *kneydlekh*, an elaborate *tsimes* like no one else could make, *kishke* and stuffed cabbage, chopped liver, noodle *kugl*, *gefilte fish* and the hot homemade mustard Sol liked with it, plus horseradish with beets mixed in for the children . . . and also sponge cake, pound cake, or honey cake, and the little chocolate cookies Myra loved, which she, Myra, had herself invented and each week helped Rivke to make: cookies made from plain sugared dough mixed with U-Bet syrup. And, in between the cooking, cleaning, so that everything should be nice for *shabes*. By the time the sun had set she would be ready to collapse – all day she had worked without pause. This was how preparing for *shabes* used to be.

Used to be, used to be, she mocked herself, looking at the frozen chicken already dripping pinkish water from the seams of its cellophane wrapping. *Still knocking on the same pot, Rivke. Used to be!* How many years, after all, had it been since this "used to be"? Many years – so many it was a miracle she could remember so well what had been, when she couldn't count on herself to remember for half an hour that she had left the water running in the bathtub. *Shabes* even before she had lost Sol had for many years not been *shabes* anymore, not what it was when she still had the children. When had she last worked a whole day *makhn shabes*? Twenty-five years ago at least – when Rachel was small and *she* was the one to help with the chocolate cookies, and Mark was only a baby: when Myra and her family were still living in Brighton, only two blocks away in a building facing the ocean, before they found a bigger apartment to move to on Homecrest Avenue, the one they lived in for – how long? – four years? five years? – before they moved away from Brooklyn altogether. When they moved to the new apartment that was farther away, Rivke understood. She knew that it was necessary for them to move – they were too crowded in the three rooms they had here; they were living as Rivke and Sol had lived: Myra and her husband sleeping on a Castro in the living room, the two children together in the bedroom. In the new apartment the children would have their own room, Myra and Harry theirs. This was as it should be, and Rivke told her daughter she was glad in her heart that she would have what Rivke had not—a room of her own to share with her husband, privacy, a door to close for a moment to have some quiet. Still, once the move was made, Rivke suffered. In her apartment it was too quiet without Myra coming in and out all day long, dropping off the children for an hour or for the afternoon; and she didn't know what to do with the days she used to spend with the children at Myra's, now that Harry no longer called to say, "Ma, can you come over this morning?"—or this evening or this afternoon— or to ask her to pick Rachel up from school or come by to give her lunch. After they moved to Homecrest Avenue, she told him again and again that she would take the bus to their new apartment, she didn't mind; she would still come and stay with the children anytime. But her son-in-law said, "We appreciate it, Ma, it's good to know, but it isn't necessary."

How was it not necessary? What was the difference? It was so much trouble to ride a bus? She told Harry, "It's no trouble for me to come to you by bus." But no, he said, it wasn't "necessary." And before they had moved, Rivke had spent entire days in their apartment, looking after the children; and for whole days the children were with *her*—often they stayed overnight. She was used to the children, and especially she was used to Rachel; from the first day that Myra had brought her home from the hospital Rivke had spent hours with the child—it was possible that she had spent more time with her in those years before the move than Myra had! She was so used to Rachel trailing around after her, hanging on to her nightgown, her housedress, her apron, asking questions, telling her long stories without taking a breath, demanding that she guess the answer to riddles, that after the child had moved with her parents and brother to the new apartment Rivke felt that a piece of her own self had been torn away. It was terrible to be separated from the child—it was worse than she had guessed. She missed her so badly sometimes that—hiding it from Sol, who did not approve of her mourning the move—she wept over it. She spent whole days remembering things Rachel had said or done; she sat for hours at a time daydreaming about the child's infancy, when she had been left with Rivke sometimes from morning till night: Rivke could see herself as she had been then, standing at the stove stirring soup with the tiny Rachel slung over her shoulder asleep.

Even when Myra came with the children on the bus to visit, it wasn't the same. And even though for a long time she came nearly every Friday night for dinner, these *shabes* meals weren't what they had been. These were visits, something different from before. Even the children knew that something had changed, and behaved differently themselves; they were polite, they sat on the couch with their ankles crossed instead of running around as they used to. Oh, little by little things changed. The years passed—and then more years passed—and suddenly she and Sol were alone more often than not, for *shabes* and otherwise. *This is life*, Rivke would tell herself on those Friday nights that she and Sol sat down to eat their *shabes* dinner alone. *Di tsayt ken alts ibermakhn*—with time everything changes. One doesn't stay busy with children forever.

And now look—look how busy: running to go lie in the bathtub. This was her preparation for *shabes*. Nothing to do but sit in the bath—and the only food in sight the yellow rock of a chicken making puddles on the counter. She gazed at it with displeasure. An ugly thing. With longing she remembered the chickens of earlier days: it used to be she could buy a fresh-killed chicken around the corner and take it home to pluck its feathers herself—and, while it was in the oven, boil the feet for Myra, who loved them, and the *pupik* for Reuben, the neck for Amos; the liver she would put under the broiler for a few minutes for Lazar; and the little pack of yolks that hadn't yet become eggs, which she had removed from inside the hen before roasting it, this was for Sammy. Everyone was happy then. And the chicken itself, when it came out of the oven, was delicious. But these chickens—today's chickens, which Myra bought for her from one of the few kosher butchers left in the neighborhood (did the Russians care about kosher?—ha) and brought home to wrap in plastic and put in the freezer—these chickens had no flavor. Not to mention no feet, no sack of eggs hidden within (Myra as a child had called them "baby eggs"), and a pathetic long-dead look and feel to them that sickened her. This chicken on the counter didn't even look to her like food. This was a rock, not a chicken. And—she realized this suddenly as she stood looking at it— this rock would never thaw out in time to be cooked before *shabes*. Hot water or no, it wouldn't be ready in time. It couldn't possibly be. She was surprised at herself for not realizing this before. Where was her head? she wondered. Then she realized something else, which surprised her even more. She didn't care one way or the other if it *didn't* thaw out in time. What if she couldn't cook the chicken today? If someone came, child or grandchild, tonight or tomorrow, he could go down to Fechter's and buy an already cooked chicken.

"So, is this such a problem?" she said, speaking directly to the frozen chicken. She shrugged. "Not such a problem, no." And, after a minute, added in a whisper that was almost a growl, "So—then . . . the hell with it."

This was the biggest surprise of all, hearing what had come out of her mouth. She stood, blinking, in the kitchen, completely astonished at herself.

Her folded clothes in a neat pile atop the tin hamper she had had since Amos's infancy (seventy years—a person's lifetime— an *old* person's lifetime, she thought, though it was a strange thing to think of her own firstborn as *old*—and she remembered perfectly the day she'd bought the hamper, Sol beside her in the store saying, "Rivke, this is a *necessary* item?"), she lay contentedly in her bath, her head resting on the air-filled plastic cushion that was shaped like a pair of lips, a recent gift from Rachel.

A bath is a marvelous thing, she thought, a joy and a comfort both— a *mekhaye*. Oh, for her it was like a cure; right now she felt wonderful. For years she had begged Sol to take baths. A bath would soothe and relax him, she had told him, but he had never had the patience for it. To sit in the water for an hour? he would say. Why should I do this? It takes me only ten minutes to get clean in the shower.

No patience. Stubborn, and no patience. But still—otherwise—a fine man, the finest. One couldn't have asked for a better husband. In the beginning, she had had some doubts about the sort of husband he would be; these were stirred up by her elder sister, who for weeks before the wedding had told her she was making a mistake. "He's an orphan," Leah had said, "which means he has already too long been too much for himself. He won't know how to do for someone else. And besides this, he is a Russian, and you know yourself what they are—hoodlums." Rivke had protested that her Sol was surely no hoodlum, he was the gentlest young man she had ever met, and that he had been hardly more than a child when he left Russia. Leah had wagged her finger. "This makes no difference. A Russian is a Russian, and a Russian is not like us. *And*, besides this, there is another matter too, which I didn't mention before because I didn't want to hurt your feelings. He is also very short. A man should be taller. Between this and that, Rivke, I frankly can't help wondering why do you need such a husband."

Rivke, making little waves with her cupped hands in the bathwater, smiled as she remembered. Ah, Leah! she thought. Look how it turned out. Short or not short (and it could not be argued that he was not short; short he was—an inch perhaps taller than she, no more), nowhere was there a man more devoted to his wife or more concerned with her welfare. The children used to in fact worry that his concern for her was so great it caused him to neglect himself. But—as he had always pointed out—*he* was healthy: about himself there was nothing to be concerned. *She* was the one who was sick, the one who had had over the years three heart attacks and had on and off been required to take all the different pills for her heart, as well as pills for her pressure, for sugar in her blood, for sourness in her stomach. She was the one who had had the operations on her eyes, her gall bladder, the veins in her legs; and it was she who for years now had had to put on every day the patches containing nitroglycerine. Naturally he worried—if it had been him, she would have worried too. "Yes, yes," the children said, "but *still*." Still, they told him, he should go once in a while to the doctor "just to be on the safe side, just to see." But if nothing was bothering him, he said, what was to see? He should go to give the doctor a chance to *find* something wrong? His only ailment, he said, was old age: the weakness of the legs and the eyes, the stiffness of the fingers, the reluctance of the bowels—all the small failures of the body that came whatever you did, however healthy. "And this," he told them, "is a sickness for which there is no help from doctors." He went once, however—once after the children would not let him alone, had kept at him for months. They had bullied him into it, he explained to Rivke, but she was sure they had frightened him into it, with their talk of something silently wrong—some illness whose signs were invisible to all but an expert. So he went, and he came back both triumphant and irritated. "Everything healthy," he announced (and Rivke, who had been in the doctor's office with him, added, "*very* healthy, remarkably healthy," which was what the doctor himself had said, for she wanted to make sure the children knew how wrong they had been). What had irritated him was all the poking and peeking. "This I didn't like," he said. "This was something humiliating, to stand so and turn so, cough now, breathe now, bend over—*feh*." He told them not to expect him to go again. And he didn't: never again did he go after this one time. Rivke understood his feelings—she hated to go too. But he *made* her go, he begged and scolded until she gave in. "What's wrong with you they'll fix," he ended by promising her each time. "Then you'll feel better." And Rachel, who for years had made it her habit to go with them in the taxi when Rivke had a doctor's appointment, agreed. "Papa's right. If there's something a doctor can do for you, you have to let him do it." "You see?" Sol would say. "She agrees with me! A smart girl, a girl with a graduate degree from college. So we'll go, and if you need medicine you'll get medicine." Oh, the faith he had in medicine! In all those pills! The best thing her new doctor (a young doctor Rachel had found for her in New York, to replace the last one Rivke had wearied of) had done for her was to take away all the pills. "Why do you want to take so many pills, Rivke?" Dr. Wagner had said to her. "You like maybe the taste?" Rivke had smiled politely and shrugged—she had no trust to spare for doctors. "Well," he said, and patted her hand—he was a nice-looking fellow, she noticed then, and twenty-five or thirty years younger than any of her previous doctors (she gave a meaningful glance over at Rachel, who refused to pay attention)—"for a young woman you're in pretty good shape, all together. So what do you say we give up these pills, stick with just the nitro patches, and see what happens. All right?" Much better than all right, Rivke told him, and—this was a surprise to her children but not to her—"what happened" was nothing. It was just as she had always suspected: the pills were worthless. The young doctor, when later she told him this, laughed and said he had often suspected as much himself. Oh, how she wished Sol could have heard this. He had thought the pills could fix anything, he had had such respect for them! "Rivke, it is time now for another pill," he used to say to her in a serious voice, as if he were an-

nouncing something of great importance. Well, it was a good
thing this Dr. Wagner had told her to stop taking all the pills,
because at this time (a year ago? maybe a little less, it was hard
to remember) she was taking three different kinds, and although
she had told no one—she had not even told Rachel—she found
that without Sol it was impossible for her to keep track of
when she was supposed to take which pill. During the years
when she had been taking so many different types of them at
once—there was a time she recalled, when there were six different kinds of pills she had to take—he had kept a chart in the
kitchen, on which he had written down what time she was
due to take each one. Then, when it was time, he would turn
up by her chair with one hand out, a pill in his palm, and
in his other hand a glass of water.

It was true that he was more concerned with her than
with himself—though it was not necessarily true that this
had always been so (the children said yes, but what children
saw was not always what was). It happened that as Sol grew
older—as they both grew older—it became truer, and in recent
years it was absolutely true, she would not deny it (why should
she deny it?). He grew older, the years passed, and with nothing else to do he became occupied with her well-being. What
else was there for him to do? He could not bear to be idle. For
a time after he had first retired he had worked at one foolish
job after another—a few months selling frankfurters on the
boardwalk, a few months standing behind the counter of a
candy store on Sixth Street, selling newspapers and cigars to
his own neighbors. This Rivke hadn't cared for at all. "You are
a hatmaker," she told him, "not a person to take from his ac-
quaintances dimes and nickels." But although after two more
jobs of this sort he finally declared himself tired of being on
his feet all day long, and said he was now looking forward to
a time of taking it easy, she saw he was restless. He went for
long walks—sometimes he walked all the way to Coney Island
before turning back—and he took an interest in household

matters that had never concerned him; he invented things to do (suddenly the toaster needed "adjustments," pictures had to be reframed "in a nicer way," the refrigerator was ready for defrosting) and he stretched chores into work: he could make a whole afternoon out of buying stamps or light bulbs. It was at this time that he began to fuss over her, insisting that she allow him to do the dishes and the laundry, brought her tea without her asking for it, draped a sweater over her shoulders if he thought she might be cold. Then came the chart for her pills—out of this he made a big project. But there wasn't anything else for him to do. He was used to working; since he was a small boy he had worked from early in the morning until night. Now he read the newspaper and took his walks, he did the shopping and the vacuuming and brought the cart full of their dirty clothes to the laundromat and sat watching them spin in the dryer, and he reminded her to take her medicine— this was his main job, he said. When she complained about having to take so many pills, he'd say to her, "Very nice, Rivke. You want to put an old man out of his job?"

He was always chasing her to give her a pill. *Always*, she thought. *Right to the end.* With a little shiver, as she lay in her bath, her head back, eyes open but useless behind the steam-clouded lenses of her glasses, she thought about the note she had found weeks after his death, after her return from Myra's house. As soon as she came upon it, stuck half-under the TV set on the kitchen table—even before she felt any surprise (or shock, which came after a moment)—she understood that it had been written the morning of the day that had ended in the hospital. He had planned to go alone to Mlotek's that morning, to leave her to sleep while he shopped: he had left the note for her to see when she woke up and came into the kitchen to put the kettle on the stove and sit down in her usual chair, by the television. But as it turned out she woke up just as he was preparing to walk out the door, and asked him to wait a while so that she could go with him. She needed

to get out also for an hour, she told him; she was tired of looking at the walls. So the note remained where he had left it and
forgotten about it, and where she would not discover it until
she sat down one day in her kitchen—weeks later, or maybe
months—to watch television for the first time since he was
gone.

> *Mayn basherter,*
> *Fargest nisht nemen* a blue pill *un leygn oyf dayn harts a*
> *nayer* patch.

It was not the reminder to take a pill and change the patch
over her heart that shocked her as she sat reading and reread-
ing the note—this was after all very familiar (it was so familiar
that she automatically reached for the bottle of the blue pills,
which at that time she was still taking for her sugar; it did not
seem to her at all strange that even then he was telling her
not to forget her medicine): it was the words by which he had
chosen to address her—*mayn basherter*, "my predestined one"—
that gave her a start. These were words, it seemed to her, that
represented a tenderness—a romantic tenderness—that was
utterly unlike him. Or—this thought came next, and unsettled
her further—if such a thing as this was "like" him, then it was
like a part of him she had never seen: a part of himself he had
kept hidden from her. For more than seventy years? Could
this be? And as she sat considering this question, another
came. She began despite herself to wonder if, somehow, on
that morning, he had *known—known* how the day would end,
known that this was his last chance to tell her something
about himself that she had never seen (that he had never allowed her to see? Or that she had only been unable to see?).
She knew it was foolish to wonder—foolish, and maybe a little
crazy—but still she did. Wondered then as now. And—sliding
lower in the bathtub to keep warm—she wondered also, now
as then, if perhaps she was not meant to take those words
so seriously. But how could she know how seriously to take

them? Not at all seriously? Only as words? If so, why *those* words? Why then?

Oh, how she had tormented herself over this—suffered so over two words on a scrap of paper! Suffered asking herself: *Was* he telling her something? What then was he telling her? And was he telling her knowing that it was his last, his only, chance to tell her?

She had never spoken to anyone about the note; no one knew it existed. Not Rachel, not Myra. Though once, just for an instant, she had been tempted to tell both of them together. She had no idea why she had *not* told—nor did she know why she had been tempted to tell them the one time she had been, on the morning of the unveiling of Sol's gravestone, exactly a year after his burial. They had come to pick her up—the car was waiting downstairs, and waiting in it were Harry, Mark and Mark's new wife—and, as she was gathering her pocketbook and keys and the sweater that Myra insisted she bring along, she felt suddenly a strong urge to speak to them of the note Sol had left. She thought she would bring them into the bedroom, take the note from the bureau drawer where it was tucked away under a stack of old linens, and show it to them; then perhaps the three of them could talk it over, and she could ask *them* what they thought. But even before she could say what she had decided to say—she meant to begin by asking if they had a minute to spare to take a look at something she had found—the impulse was gone, leaving her as mysteriously as it had come to her, and she wanted only to get out of the apartment, into the car, and to the cemetery as quickly as possible. More than anything she wished to get the unveiling itself over with—it was at that moment that she realized how much she was dreading the ceremony.

It occurred to her now, as she struggled to sit up in her cooling bath—she wanted to pull the stopper to let out a little of the lukewarm water and add fresh hot water from the tap—that before long it would be a year since that day. *This* year, thank God, they would not mark the anniversary of his death—she was very grateful for this. The unveiling, as she had guessed it would be only minutes before setting out for it, had been hard on her. It was a ceremony for which she had no use, an affair designed only to stir up unhappiness. Yet it was not the pointlessness of it that had made it so difficult to bear. Nor was it seeing, finally, the stone Amos had ordered (this was hard on her, naturally—just returning to the gravesite was hard, and seeing it marked now with the square of stone into which Sol's name had been carved was worse than that— was something like a nightmare); no, more disturbing still was the behavior of her children on that day. It was not even that they behaved *badly* (they were not, after all, children; they were parents and grandparents themselves). It was only that they behaved—so she told herself afterwards—exactly as she had *expected* they would. Or, rather, as she *would* have expected if she had given any thought to it, which she had not. There was no need to think of expectations where her children were concerned: they were always the same. And she? Perhaps she was the fool, she reflected. For she was always disappointed.

Lazar as usual had been late—when had he ever *not* been late? she asked herself with a shake of her head. A scatter of cold water rang from the ends of her hair onto her shoulders, and, shivering, she submerged herself again and thrust her feet directly under the tap, from which rushed new hot water. Oh, Lazar! she thought sadly. Always late or else missing altogether. His arrival even to life had been late, delayed from the start: her longest labor had been with him (though not her most painful, her most painful had been with Amos). Naturally, for the unveiling of his father's stone, he had kept everyone waiting until nearly an hour after the service had been scheduled to begin. Rivke remembered perfectly well how they had all stood around the grave, fidgeting and perspiring, the less-known relations wondering in loud whispers what was holding things up, and Rivke's children and grandchildren shrugging and looking first at the sky and then at the ground. Only the rabbi seemed not to mind the wait. *And why should he mind?* Rivke recalled whispering to Rachel. *For this he's getting paid a hundred and seventy-five dollars.* A hundred and seventy-five dollars! Rivke still could not get over it. It was her nephew Meyer, newly turned orthodox in the year following Sol's death, who had insisted she hire the tiny, stooped Hasid with his foot-long gray beard. But she had put up only the most feeble of arguments over this—feeble because none of her own children had stepped forward to engage the services of a rabbi, and she was grateful for Meyer's help. Still—she marveled over it even now—a hundred and seventy-five dollars!

They had all stood under the sun waiting for Lazar, and Rivke with a wave of her hand refused again and again the offers to take her back to one of the cars, where she could sit and even, if she chose, have air conditioning. No, she said to them, please, I'm fine right here. But Mama, they said, it's such a hot day. Yes, she agreed politely, it was a hot day, it was true the sun was very strong, but still she preferred to stand and wait with the rest of them. She stood in fact a little apart from them, her children; she stood close to Rachel, holding firmly to her arm, and they whispered together about this and that to pass the time. Then finally there was Lazar, running toward them over the grass, making circles around the tombstones but trampling on graves without noticing what he was doing. Behind him was his shrew of a wife, walking slowly, a big white hat flapping unevenly around her face. From far away she was yelling, "Hello, hello everybody, sorry we're late." When she approached the place where they were gathered, she came right away to Rivke and kissed her cheek with her dry lips. Loudly, she said, "I shouldn't even be here, out in the sun like this. My doctor would kill me." She waited for Rivke to ask her what was wrong, but Rivke smiled and nodded, pretending she hadn't understood.

"Why are you always late?" Rivke heard Samuel say behind her. "Even on a day like this you have to be late? You're not ashamed?" Lazar muttered that he was sorry, and Rivke turned away from Naomi—her voice was enough to give her a headache, let alone what she might say—in time to see Lazar hug his youngest brother and take his place in the jagged semicircle around the grave. Samuel, for some reason, had a problem the opposite of Lazar's—he was always early. On this day he had been waiting, leaning against his car, when Harry and Myra's car pulled up. His wife, he announced as he helped Rivke out of the back seat, would be coming later with the younger of his two daughters. Nobody asked him why it was necessary for him and his wife to take two separate cars to the cemetery, just as nobody asked where his son and other daughter were. Too many questions, it didn't pay to ask. But Rivke looked at him carefully as they walked together to the grave. He looked not well. Too many years of waiting—this was what she thought. For years he had waited, and nothing ever came to him. She had seen from the back seat of the car, from a long way away as Harry drove up the path to this part of the cemetery, how miserable he was, waiting. He had a forlorn look like someone's puppy left outdoors. This was her Samuel, the youngest of her sons, the one she had named after her father: always the first to be anywhere. When you reached a place you were going to, you would see first Sammy before anything else—Sammy standing hunched over waiting near his car, or leaning against a wall, or looking worried out a window, ready to ask you where you'd been for so long. But here was another thing: even though he had been the first to arrive at the cemetery and had had to wait, he said, for more than an hour for anyone else to get there, he hung back unhelpfully once the others came. He didn't greet the cousins, he didn't go up to speak to the rabbi, and when Amos and Myra began to unload the trunks of their cars, he stood like a block of wood and didn't move a muscle to help them—which was just as well, for he would have been more upset than they were when it turned out the work was for nothing, when, after they had removed nearly everything from both cars, Harry, who had stood by silently until then, remarked that they really ought to put it all back in, out of sight, until after the service.

"Why?" Myra said, stopping with her arms full of boxes of *babka* and cookies. One long strand of hair dangled across her face—she had no hand free to reattach it to the golden-frosted coil atop her head—and she was breathing hard from the effort of having made so many trips from the car to the bridge table she and Amos had set up across the gravel path from Sol's grave.

"Because it isn't a good idea to have this set up while the service is going on, that's why. It doesn't look nice."

Rivke looked then at the table. It looked nice enough to her, in a circle of shade-darkened grass under a short tree full of white flowers; if you didn't look much past the tree you might not notice the stones that studded the grass beyond it. The table was covered with a red cloth and piled with stacked-up paper plates and napkins and boxes of sweet things; there were also towers of plastic shotglasses and an enormous bottle of *shnaps* on a swinging stand.

"Well, why didn't you say so earlier?" Myra said. But she didn't sound angry. Rivke watched with interest as she began to reload the trunk with the boxes she was holding. Amos watched too for a while, then joined in himself, going to the table and bringing back an armful of cakeboxes, which he deposited in the back seat of his car. His wife, Frances, who had not yet stirred from the front seat (her legs hurt especially badly today, she had told Rivke, speaking in a confidential tone through the open window of the car), paid no attention to the activity around her; she went on speaking to Amos about matters unrelated to the business at hand—a grandchild's report card, a roast she planned to fix for dinner when they returned home that evening, another grandchild's recent case of measles—and Rivke noticed that as she spoke she did not once look at her husband or adjust the volume of her voice as he moved from car to table and back again. Was Amos listening? Rivke wondered. He didn't speak a word in response.

And, bit by bit, Myra stopped speaking too. From the moment she began to reload everything she had just finished unloading (including the table—which, its legs once again collapsed beneath it, appeared to be much more difficult to replace than it had been to withdraw), she became quieter and quieter: a few words here, a word there, and then silence. Silence, in any case, was what she offered Rivke; if she had words for anyone else, Rivke didn't hear them and couldn't have heard them, since Myra stayed far from her for the rest of the day. It seemed to Rivke, in fact, that her daughter was purposely keeping away from her. Could she be imagining this? Myra stood by relatives she had met just once or twice before—while Amos, who usually preferred to keep to himself, surprised Rivke by coming to stand beside her at the start of the service and remaining there, his hand on her arm squeezing so tight it felt to her like he was taking her blood pressure. When she looked up at him he looked back with solemn eyes, he nodded at her and he squeezed harder, but he didn't have anything to say either.

Nobody speaking! What was wrong with her children? Even Reuben, who always had something to say, wasn't talking. He was too busy to talk—he was busy with his little granddaughter (what was her name? something very silly—Candy or Randy or Brandy, a word that was not a name). He was so busy with the child that he had to be called three times by the rabbi before he came to stand with the rest of them when the service began. And on such a day why wasn't the child's mother taking care? Where *was* the child's mother? Not at the cemetery. What kind of a mother was the girl, Ruby's daughter? And why did Ruby stand for such nonsense? Before the

birth of this fatherless baby (oh, she had a father, Candy-
Brandy—she had a father someplace, and sometimes the father lived with the two of them, the mother and the child,
and sometimes not; each time he moved out, Julia and the little girl moved in again with Reuben), no one would have believed that he could become so busy with a child. With his
own children he had never been so busy. Always he had been
involved with something—some new business, something.
And money, always money. This had been, Rivke thought, his
main interest. But no more. Now it was the child he was interested in. Who would have guessed this could be?

Still, from all the years of business, he was the wealthiest
of her children—this the others told her. Also (this she could
see for herself) he was the handsomest. Though not as tall as
Amos, he looked to Rivke somehow taller, with his big chest,
his shirt open to show hair there. And the hair on his head,
still black (but perhaps he dyed it?—he was after all past sixty),
was pushed back flat and puffed up high in front like a movie
star's. Oh, he was handsome, with his suntan and his voice
like an actor's voice, loud and happy. Whether he was really
happy, Rivke couldn't tell. He didn't talk about it. Did anyone
know what was in his heart? The rumor among the other
children, Rivke had been told years ago, was that his wife
(who was of course not at the unveiling, since she wanted
nothing to do with Rivke; she had not come with her husband to the funeral either) played around with men, and that
he no longer cared. Rivke didn't know—she didn't wish to
know—if this was true or not true. She knew enough about
her children, as far as she was concerned; she didn't need to
know anything else.

In her mind she lined up the children this way: there was
first serious Amos—who had been as a boy the most rebellious
of them and the most difficult, but who had long ago rid from
himself every last bit of rebelliousness; he was now, as he had
been for years, a big, solid, silent man, full of secrets. To whom

did Amos tell his secrets? Not to his wife, Rivke was sure. And to her, to his own mother, he was a stranger—she knew enough to know, always, what he was going to say before he said it. But as he didn't have so much to say, how much, she wondered, did she really know?

After Amos was clumsy, worried Lazar, forever late and forever sorry; busy, handsome Reuben, her noisiest child from birth till now, who though he had plenty to say was always in such a big hurry he could never sit still and say it for more than a minute; anxious Sammy, too eager, always too early, who had failed so often in business, Rivke had been told, that his brother Reuben now practically supported him; and fragile Myra—the most nervous and the most sensitive of the children, who was as brittle, Rivke thought, as a piece of glass, and who like glass could seem to disappear into what was around and beyond her, vanishing so thoroughly it sometimes was as if she were hardly in the world at all.

Oh. Rivke groaned, and blinking as if she had just woken up, looked around her at the grayish tiles and the white-handled faucets stamped hot and cold; at the shower curtain, with its pattern of blue and gray swans, bunched up near the front of the tub; at the cool water in which she lay and her own pink feet and knees beneath its surface. *Oh*—she groaned again and shook her head—what was wrong with her? When had she ever made such a catalogue of her children—a list of their faults and peculiarities, their worst traits? This was not what she truly felt about them. She had become overwrought, she thought, thinking too much and for too long about what she shouldn't be thinking about. She loved her children and knew that they were *good*, all of them. They had problems, naturally they had problems—the whole world had problems. Their lives had been difficult. Unreasonably difficult, Rivke thought, and much of their difficulties seemed to have to do with the marriages they had made. Why they had made such poor matches, she couldn't say. But for this, for making such a mistake, you couldn't condemn a child. No—her heart was full of sympathy for them. She was guilty, she felt, of remembering too much of what was bad, not enough of what was good. As she had sat in her tub recalling the day Sol's gravestone had been unveiled, what she had forgotten to think about was her love for her children. Of course she loved them! That day, every day! Yes, perhaps it was true that she had once expected more from them. When they were children, she had expected more. But they had been adults for much longer than they had been children, and who could hold against them what was now ancient history? Who after all was likely to change anymore once childhood was left behind? How could she hold against them what was true for the world? She didn't. She held nothing against them. She remembered standing at the grave that day amost a year ago and looking at them one by one as the rabbi talked; she had noticed how unhappy they all looked, and she had remarked to herself—perhaps she had even whispered to Rachel—that the rabbi was evidently doing his job. She saw them grieving; she felt for them. And if she had not been able to help thinking that she was the one who had suffered the greatest loss, was this not natural? She wanted to be comforted by her chidren—she wanted recognition of the ineffability of her loss. But she knew that it was their loss too—her heart was not hard to this. If their loss was less than hers, and their grief, it did not mean that theirs was not great.

Ach. Impatiently (impatient with whom? she asked herself. With herself, or with her children? Or only with these thoughts that led to nothing?), she took hold of the sides of the tub and pulled herself forward so that she was sitting up straight. It was time to soap and rinse herself so that she could get out —she had had enough of this bath. She removed her glasses and set them down on the lid of the toilet, beside the tub. As her hands returned to the water, burrowing there and emerging with cupped palms holding pools of water, she was overwhelmed suddenly with a feeling she could not even name – part grief, part bitterness. She cried out, the pain that came with it was so sharp.

For what? she thought. For what was all her life? What did it amount to? To her children? Look at her children.

Without glasses Rivke couldn't see anything – patches of blurred colors and light only – and she looked around in confusion at the nothing she was able to see. *How did it come out to this? How did this happen?*

Sol, she thought, *how could you have left me to finish by myself?*

The same way he always left you – this was the answer that came to her at once from another part of her. *The same like he did all your life together.* Rivke blinked and shivered, wondering: true? *Yes, it's true. Now maybe he's not here, but what was he before – here?*

Here, she thought, but also not here. And this had nothing to do with love. He had loved her – oh, he had always loved her! – but he had left, always, all the business of life to her. He couldn't be bothered with it. And what would his answer be to the question of what it had all been for? "Ah, Rivke," he would say, "why do you ask questions for which there is no answer? It was for what it was for."

"You're right." She said this out loud. "Absolutely you're right. I would be better off not asking questions like this. But if a question comes, it comes, and better off or not better off I want to know an answer." She noticed that she sounded very calm. She did not feel calm. In her chest there was a slamming like a drawer being opened and closed many times, too roughly, in quick succession. "An answer!" she said. Her voice was hoarse and it echoed in the small, tiled room. "I want to know this. If for you and for the children I gave away my whole life, I want to know what did I do it for? What do I have to show for it?"

It made her uneasy, hearing her words bouncing back at

her. Sol had often scolded her for talking to herself. "Does this make sense to you, to talk to the walls?" he used to say. 'What kind of person talks to walls, to windows, to furniture? Talking is good only when you can get an answer." "Is that so?" she would say—and that was all she would say; she wouldn't argue. Now she told him, "Maybe then I shouldn't have talked to *you*. From you I received an answer only half the time."

No response from him now, either, of course. Like then.

"Some things, you never understood. For example, that a person needs sometimes to talk only to talk, only to hear herself. You could have done worse yourself than to talk to walls—at least you would have been talking. You preferred to keep quiet altogether."

But it was possible—was it possible?—that this had been her own fault. It could be that she had not tried hard enough to get him to talk. And to listen also? Long ago she had ceased to expect answers from him; also long ago she had given up telling him anything of importance. She had fallen into the habit of speaking to him only of things that didn't matter one way or the other—then, when he didn't answer, that didn't matter either. For years—for decades—she had made no attempt to talk out what was on her mind.

"To tell you the truth," she said in a whisper, hoping the whisper would fool the tiled walls into silence, "there were many things I would have liked to say."

The whisper echoed just like all the other words, and, despondent, she sat with her arms crossed over her chest, hugging herself—she was trembling; the bathwater was by now quite cold—and wondering what it was exactly that she had meant to tell him. Was there something in particular about herself that she had once intended to say? She couldn't think of what it might have been. Well, she thought, irritated, how could she know now? The time to speak had passed—it had passed long ago. She should have spoken up then, while it was on her mind; she should have talked and talked until he had no choice but to listen to her, she should have forced him to listen until he had no choice but to respond. This was what she should have done.

And if she had? What if she had? What if she had *made* him listen, made him talk? What if she had *fought* him? She had never fought him. She had let things be, she had kept quiet.

When she was a child she had been taught that it was better, always, to be quiet than to speak—this was her father's lesson. "Words can do harm," he used to say. When he heard her quarreling with her mother, he would hush her, and he would hush her also when he heard her telling her younger brothers what she thought of them. Never mind that her mother had just taken back her promise to hire a tutor for her, so that she might learn to read and write Hebrew; never mind that Reuven and Yischak had been teasing *her* and had driven her to lash out at them in her own defense. Her father, gentle man, heard Rivke tell her mother that she was mean, he heard her tell her brothers that she wished they'd never been born, and he came flying into the room to snatch her away and warn her that she would be sorry later for yielding to the desire to utter such words. "Rivke," he told her, "it would be better to keep thoughts like this to yourself." *He* kept thoughts like this, he said (but did he have such thoughts? It was hard to imagine), to himself. "Think every time before you speak," he told her, "and you'll see you don't really want to put the thought into words after all, because if you do, you'll regret later the damage. Words can do much harm, Rivkeleh." But words could also do more than harm—worse than harm. They could also do nothing. This her father hadn't mentioned; she had figured this out by herself. Early in her marriage she had learned that for her the nothing was more terrible than the harm. What had kept her from speaking her mind all those years was not fear that she might regret having said what should have remained unsaid, but dread of the more likely possibility—that what she said would have no effect at all.

And so she had kept her thoughts to herself. And if she had not—what then? What if she *had* spoken? What in her life would have been altered?

She didn't even have to ask the question; she knew the answer. Nothing would have been altered. This was plain to her. Whatever had been would have been; what had happened would have happened. It was not words spoken or unspoken that made the difference—this made no difference. All the talk in the world changed nothing.

And now it came to her, suddenly, how hopeless was the plan she had hatched concerning the missing beads, the beads which—she now realized—she had not thought of in days. Days? Weeks. How long? "Two weeks," she muttered, guessing. She hadn't the slightest idea. But for however long it had been, it had just now occurred to her that she was waiting— had *been* waiting, thinking or not thinking about it—to hear from her grandson as if talking to him would solve the problem. As if a problem could be solved with words!

How had she convinced herself that talking to Mark was the solution? What had she been thinking of, she wondered, to imagine that this was all that was necessary? Surely she knew better. She did know better. "Talk!" She spit the word as if it were a curse. She felt disgusted with herself. Of what earthly use was talk?

She sat shivering—she was shivering so hard she could hear her jaw rattling—and berating herself. *Foolish old woman!* What had she thought: "I'll just talk to the boy and everything will turn out all right"? Was she really capable of such simple-minded self-deception? She hissed at herself. *You're a fool, Rivke.* And what if, by some miracle, her plan did "work" in the way she had imagined it would? What if it did result in the return of the beads? What good would it do? It would do no good! Even if the beads were returned, it would never be the same. She would always know that they had been taken from her.

Abruptly she reached down, beneath her feet, and pulled the plug from the drain. She had to get out of the bathtub, she thought; if she didn't, she would turn to ice. Still, she spent a minute listening to the quiet, sucking sound the water made as it began to leave the tub. She closed her eyes. Just the thought of the effort that was ahead filled her with despair. It seemed impossible that she would manage it today. But she would; she would manage it, she told herself grimly. She had no choice, there was no other way out.

Thus—with a sigh so deep it felt to her as if it had taken from her chest every last bit of her breath—she began to inch forward. *Carefully*, she told herself. *Little by little. Take your time.*

6

She was cleaning, for *shabes* — doing, anyway, what passed now for cleaning: raising pale clouds of dust from the couch cushions as she smacked them with her broom, slapping a feather duster at the venetian blinds, passing a strip of torn pillowcase over end tables and windowsills.

From living room to bedroom she proceeded at the pace of a snail — this she remarked to herself without bitterness; it was not in the least unpleasant to move through her rooms this way, the feather duster tucked under one arm, the broom under the other, the dustpan and rag in hand, taking her small steps with a pause between each to draw in a breath. She felt not so bad now. She had had a nap after her bath, and then a cup of tea with lemon; now she felt she was accomplishing something, however slowly. As she worked, her mind was busy with a series of questions and answers, in singsong: Would the chicken not be ready in time to cook it? Well, then, so what? Would she not be able to make the house really clean? Of course she wouldn't, but who cared? Was it likely that she would once again spend *shabes* alone, that no one would come either tonight or tomorrow, that no one in fact would come all weekend long? If yes, what did it matter?

And, as she cleaned, the preparation for *shabes* made her think of the holiday for which preparations would also soon have to be made. For this, for making things ready for *peysekh*, she would need Rachel's help. The dishes had to be changed over, a big job — the two sets of everyday dishes moved to the highest cabinets and the once-a-year glass dishes to the more accessible shelves over the sink. Also, she thought, for *peysekh* it might not be such a bad idea to hire a person to thoroughly clean the apartment. Myra had been after her for a long time to do this, and she had to admit that to have everything clean for the holiday would be nice.

But what sort of holiday would it be? This was hard to guess. That there would be no proper observance this year was a pity—they used to celebrate *peysekh* so beautifully. It was Sol's holiday; it was the perfect holiday on which to celebrate his birthday, Rivke had always said. Such pleasure it gave him to make a seder! He used to supervise everything. For this occasion he even put himself in charge of her cooking, telling her what to fix, in what order to serve it, how to arrange the platters on the table. Once a year, she didn't mind—it was so pleasantly startling to see him in such a state of enjoyment. For days beforehand he rushed around giving her orders, counting *Hagadahs*, shopping, worrying. Everything, he said, had to be *just so*. He was all over the neighborhood buying the nicest fruit, the fattest chicken, the most beautiful walnuts and almonds; he polished and polished again the silver cup he would use for the seder, as well as the tray on which it rested all year long. After the children were grown, he would telephone them over and over to remind them that the seder was less than a week away, was in only three days, was tomorrow. Then, when the night came, with what feeling did he read aloud to them the story of bondage and flight, the psalms and the prayers, the answers to the four questions! But it was the singing he loved most, and when it came time for this everyone else kept his voice low, to better hear him. He sang, as it happened, very badly—even he knew how badly, and every year he turned it into a joke, asking the children if they thought he ought to give up the millinery business and become a *khazen*, singing in the *shul*—but it made everyone happy to listen to him because *he* was so happy: his joy gave them theirs. He smiled and sang at the same time, and his face as he sang became redder and redder, his voice grew louder, and perspiration began to shine where he no longer had hair on his head. Soon tears came also (and Rivke, who had waited for this moment from the beginning of the seder, as she waited for it each year, marveled over it: for how often did she see her husband cry?) and then he was crying *and* smiling as he sang—a result, thought Rivke, of sweet wine and emotion both.

Oh, it was a good occasion, happy always. She used to tell him every year after it was over—after the dishes had been cleaned and put away, the gifts of neckties and handkerchiefs (and, later, gold cufflinks and bottles of expensive *shnaps*) opened and exclaimed over, the tattered copies of the *Hagadah* stacked in a drawer for next year—that it was lucky for him his birth had occurred nearest to this of all possible holidays.

Her own birthday had been marked, the year she was born, by Yom Kippur, the day for making amends for one's sins and appealing to God for forgiveness. Was there anywhere on the calendar a worse day for a birthday? This was *her* luck. As a child she had been dolefully resigned to it—to the necessary solemnity of the day, the absence of celebration, the fasting and the hours of prayer inside the dark *shul* while outdoors it was bright, first-cold autumn—but when she was a little older she began to feel resentful. Since the day was an arbitrary one (for no record existed of the actual day of her birth—of anyone's birth at that time and in that place), her mother, she decided, *could* have picked another. It came to her then that perhaps it had been meant as a kind of joke—a mean joke, one of her mother's many small cruelties. But quickly she talked herself out of this suspicion. No mother, she thought, could be so monstrous. And yet the *feeling* stuck—the sense that the birthday had been selected purposefully—and when she was older still, after she had left Poland, she found herself in America wondering (idly, but still—to wonder was to wonder) if there was supposed to be a message in it. Who, she asked herself, had her mother meant to be paying for what sins?

Sol, when she first met him, made his own joke about her birthday. On the day when one made peace with God, he said, one had also to make peace with Rivke. "To God we pray," he told her, "and to Rivkeleh we bring gifts, and in this way peace is restored all around." This not only did not seem to her something to smile about, it annoyed her so much she felt for a while less affection for him on the whole. Still, it was he who had the idea, some months after he had made his joke, that they assign the day *before* the Day of Atonement to be her birthday. "Where is it written that a birthday has to be celebrated precisely on a holiday?" he asked her. "Because someone remembers that you were born sometime near Yom Kippur doesn't mean on Yom Kippur, and if we're going to make you a birthday it might as well be a happier one."

Of course, this—the day that preceded Yom Kippur—was no day for light-hearted pleasure either: it was a day designated to be set aside for peacemaking with everyone *other* than God, a day for forgiving those with whom one had quarreled and visiting with the dead. Nevertheless, it was better than the day that followed. At least, as Sol told her, on this day one could eat a meal in her honor and have a drink to her health.

He was the one who knew what was allowable and what was not, for she was not herself a seriously observant Jew. Oh, she kept a kosher home, naturally, and she lit candles for *shabes* and attended to the holidays as she had been taught long ago, in the old country; but except for funerals, *bar mitzves*, or weddings she could not remember the last time she had stepped foot in *shul*. It was Sol who attended services regularly, and once in a while he would criticize her for her lack of religious feeling. This made her angry. "Feeling," she would say, "I have plenty of, more than enough." It wasn't *feeling* he really meant, she told him; no, it seemed to her that what he thought she was lacking was a certain seriousness about the *rules* of feeling. And she told him, "There is a saying that goes like this: It's better to be good than to be pious." This was something which in her childhood she had often heard her mother tell her father. She could not recall what her father's answer had been; Sol's was to shrug and say, mildly, "No one is asking you to make a choice between the two."

He complained also about the way she talked to God. "I hear you talking," he said, "and praying it isn't. To God you speak as if He were your upstairs neighbor. A personal ac-quaintance! Is this right, Rivke? To me this isn't right." But she had no particular interest in whether it was right or not right. It was comfortable: this was the main thing. If she did what was comfortable, she felt, she couldn't go wrong. Thus, while it was comfortable to do what she had been taught to do as a girl—to keep separate dishes for milk and meat, to make spe-cial meals for celebrations, to stop work for *shabes*—in the finer points of the Law she had no interest. It was too much work, she told him, to keep track of so many rules. And who had time for extra work? "I have no time for it," she told him frankly. He disliked very much to hear her say this. But the code she lived by, she thought, based on custom and good sense, had served her well, simple as it was; and without all the fuss and the talk of this and that, she pointed out, she was a good Jew. Well, wasn't she? she asked him. Wasn't she a good wife, a good mother? Wasn't *this* the real test, not how many prayers she knew by heart? It was she who raised the children, taught them right from wrong. This was what counted in the end—didn't he agree? Did he want to have an argument with her over who was the better Jew? Would he be that silly, that petty? (But this she didn't say, she only thought it. Much of this argument, in fact, it seemed to her now, as she went over it, had been unspoken: her own private fight with him, waged in silence, her mind answering what she knew was in his mind.)

Who was to say what made one a good Jew? After all it was she and not he who had wanted for years—who had begged!-

to visit the Holy Land. *He* was the one who wouldn't go; it was she who had a strong desire to see a place where everyone was a Jew. "Every person on the street!" she had told him. "Doesn't it seem to you that this would be something worth seeing?" Had she ever received an answer to this question? She couldn't remember. What she did remember was that every year she had asked him, "Next year we can go?" and each time he had said no, not next year. He spoke of the expense, the time involved, the children (the children! As if leaving the children was an issue once they were all grown and married!), and, finally, of the possible danger ("Bombs, Rivke," he told her, "bombs and guns. This you don't think about, but in Israel there is always war"). And yet the plain truth, she knew, was that the real reason, the only reason, he wouldn't take her to the promised land was that he was afraid to fly.

About this too they had argued, many times. He would not get on an airplane—he would not *consider* getting on an airplane—and he would not admit, either, that he was afraid. He would only say no. And what was the reason? "Because no is no." This was his answer. But she knew he was afraid. It was because of his fear that on the one real vacation they had ever taken—this was to Miami, years ago—they had gone by train. "Everyone else in the world flies," she had said to him bitterly when finally they arrived in Florida. "For the rest of the world, it's an hour, two hours, and they're where they're going. Not us. *We* have to sit for a whole day and a night with our bones rattling. *Next* time," she told him, "no matter what you say"—a promise to herself—"we fly also. Like everyone."

But there wasn't a next time, which was no surprise, and so, because *he* was afraid, she had never had a chance to fly. And she was not only not afraid, she *wanted* to do it, she was very curious about it. But when she said to him, "Don't you wonder even a little bit what it would be like?" his answer was still only no. No, no, and again no. But why *not*? she asked him. *How* not? Because not, he said. Not means not, and that's that.

But still she wanted to do it. Even now—she still wanted to see what it was like. And could she? she wondered. Was that possible? Still? Could she ask Rachel to take her sometime on a plane? Oh, not necessarily to Israel—her taste for that trip had diminished over the years, and in any case it didn't seem to her likely that Rachel would be interested—but somewhere. Anywhere. California? Or France. Or Mexico. Hawaii.

Rivke paused, feather duster in hand, at the bedroom window, picturing herself and Rachel in some faraway place. She saw them in a restaurant: they were sitting together at a table in front of a wall made of glass. The ocean, she imagined, lay somewhere beyond the glass—yes, the ocean and a beach; and, before the beach, right outside the restaurant, was a street crowded with people clothed in bright colors (*costumes*, she thought, *native dress*), speaking to each other in a foreign language. Near the ocean she put a boardwalk, with shops along it on the street side, and benches opposite the shops. She set a railing in front of the benches, separating boardwalk from beach. On the railing, children played, hanging on the bars . . . and their mothers, sitting on the benches, scolded them to get away before they fell. Also on the benches sat old people, some alone, some not—and here and there others walked, in pairs and in threes, arms linked, their canes tapping loudly on the wood planks. . . .

And now, suddenly, she stopped—she was laughing at herself. *Brighton Beach*, she thought. Brighton Beach in France. In Mexico. In Hawaii.

Very good, Rivke. You've imagined for yourself what's just outside the door.

Well, and how much less impossible was it for her to take a walk along the boardwalk here, a few blocks from her own door, than to take a trip to Hawaii, to Mexico? *Mexico!* Sure Mexico! This is just what I need, she told herself wryly as she resumed dusting the blinds. A trip! Sure a trip. And what did one do on a trip? One went strolling, sightseeing. And how

was she supposed to stroll and see sights when she couldn't
walk any more than the little bit of walking she did around
the apartment? Her legs were too weak to take her farther
than a city block—at *most*, now, a city block. One of her doctors, a long time ago, had told her that it was a good thing
her legs were so weak: they kept her from going farther than
her heart could bear. This remark had made a great impres-
sion on Sol, who for years afterwards had repeated it. "Isn't
that something?" he would say. "Your legs save your heart.
One part of the body looks out for another."

The bedroom finished—or as finished as it could be—she
emptied the dustpan into the tin wastebasket which had stood
in this corner of the room since the first week she had lived
in the apartment, and once again she stuck the feather duster
under one arm, the broom under the other; the rag went into
the deep pocket of her apron (an apron she had made for herself long ago, out of red-and-black checked dimity left over from
a dress she remembered making for Myra when she started high
school; the pocket was a rectangle of black velvet Sol had
brought home from the factory). She moved on now to the
bathroom. Here there was not much, in fact, that she could
do—she stood considering doubtfully the toilet and the tub—
but still, she told herself, she could do *something*: she could
always do something.

She swept the small square of floor (this didn't take long,
a minute or two only) and ran hot water into the sink; she
spent another minute splashing the water around with her
hand. Next she used the rag to carefully wipe the mirror. How
many thousands of times had she wiped this mirror in just
such a way! Wiped this mirror, swept this floor. How many
minutes of her life, she wondered, had been spent thus? Week
after week, year after year, sweeping this same patch of tiles.
A minute, two minutes a week for more than sixty years . . .
thousands of minutes, and to do what? To sweep a floor! And
in the old days she had always taken a mop to it, too, after

the sweeping was done. Ten minutes more, then. All those hours spent on this little bit of floor! So much time that could have been spent otherwise, spent better. It was *now*—now, when she had nothing better to do, nothing *else* to do—that she should be washing floors. And it was now that she couldn't. Another one of life's tricks.

It was a strange business to live long enough to become unable to do the work that had at one time been second nature, automatic. She thought now of her mother, who had seemed old at the end of her life, but had not lived long enough for this—had not lived to see herself grow really old, incapable of work. Right to the end, Mina had managed. Of course, she had managed mainly—Rivke recalled with a snort—to make a nuisance of herself. She had in her mind a picture of her mother in the kitchen, removing all the dishes and pots from the cabinets and setting them down on the floor in great stacks, stacks which blocked Rivke's way to her stove and icebox: she was clearing out the cabinets, Mina explained, so that she could scrub the insides of them. *This* was how she kept herself busy during the time she lived with Rivke. Scrubbing out cabinets, washing windows. Dusting, also. Oh, and she used to scour the bathtub! Remembering, Rivke groaned. Sixty-seven years old, and she used to climb inside the bathtub and for an hour— for two hours—rub and scrape it as if it were filthy. And was it filthy? It was never filthy.

Rivke glanced now into the tub (which was clean enough, just as it was, for her) and gave her head a shake to clear it of the vision of her mother on hands and knees with the scrub brush. Crazy, to work so hard at a job that must have been by then painful to do. Certainly it could not have been easy. Not anymore, not at that age. But still she did it; as long as she *could* do it, she did it. Well, and this Rivke understood herself—for when had *she* given up such work? When it became impossible, only. Not before. She recalled herself at sixty-seven, at seventy—at seventy-five!—still cleaning, still knocking herself out. And still telling herself she could "manage": could manage to clean, could manage to shop, could manage to take a walk with Sol on the boardwalk, though the walks she managed then were not very long—the equivalent perhaps of a few blocks—and required frequent and not brief rests, so that the truth was they spent more time sitting on benches watching the ocean than they did walking. But could you admit a thing like this? Not until you had to—not until the time came when you had no choice, because all at once everything was becoming impossible. How could you insist that you could still take walks by the ocean when you couldn't anymore push a mop across your own bathroom floor?

But until then, until the choice had been made for you, it was necessary to refuse to give in. So, for this—for this refusal—could she blame her mother? No, she couldn't blame her. She had sympathy for her. *Now*, remembering, she had sympathy. Not then. *Then* she had complained to Sol that her mother was trying to humiliate her, to point out how dirty her home was, to let her know that she, Mina, was a superior housekeeper, a superior person. And this had most likely been true: her mother *had* been doing everything possible to humiliate and antagonize her. That was Mina's way, exactly so. But was it *less* true, then, that there was something else at stake also, something besides the battle (begun when? the day Rivke was born?) she was fighting with her? Not less true, no. True the same amount. It was a revelation—this idea that both things could be true at the same time. But how could Mina *not* have been involved in her own, altogether separate battle? One against inability, infirmity. Against nothingness, Rivke thought. Like *her* own battle. Against everything.

It struck her suddenly that between what she did know (only so few things, it seemed to her now: only that Mina had disliked her and had been grimly, angrily resigned to the prospect of living out what was left of her life in Rivke's home) and what she did not (anything—everything—else about what

Mina had felt and thought), there could be in fact many explanations for her behavior during the final months of her
life. Contradictory explanations. *And all true?* All true, Rivke
thought. All true at the same time.

But how could this be? It was very confusing—the whole
business was confusing. With so many—too many—things to
take into account, how could you believe you *knew* anything?
She stood, disturbed, hands resting on the sink, facing the little mirror she had wiped clean so many thousands of times,
and at once another thought, no less disturbing, came to her.
Wasn't it possible, if such a variety of truths existed, that if
Mina had lived long enough, different things would have *become* true? That—in other words—Mina might have changed?

Oh, impossible to imagine Mina changed! Changed how?
Changed how and still be Mina? But—Rivke worked it out
slowly, her eyes on the mirror—what if she *had* lived long
enough to discover that there were things she couldn't do?
Would not such a revelation have softened her? Humbled her?

She closed her eyes now as she tried to see this: her mother
humbled, admitting—admitting to *her*—that there was something which on her own she couldn't manage. Her mother asking for her help, accepting her help—her mother grateful.

No, she thought, it was impossible, it was too unlike her.
But *wasn't* it possible (Ah, *so stubborn!* she thought. Such stubborn ideas!) that, had Mina lived, she would have changed
in precisely such a way that it would not any longer have *been*
unlike her? Surely, Rivke told herself, if one lived long enough,
anything was possible. All things might be true; all things
might be possible.

But now, strangely—for she had never known her—it was
of Sol's mother whom she thought. *Zipporah*—Rivke tested
aloud the sound of the name—who had died when still a
young woman. Zipporah, wife of Amos, mother of Sol, who
was only a baby at the time of her death; Zipporah who had
not lived long enough for anything to be possible.

About her Rivke knew not a thing besides her name and the single, cold fact that she had lived to bear six children and then to vanish from the earth, taken by an illness that took also her husband, her eldest son, and her next-to-eldest daughter. Sol of course had never known his mother. Only Etke, the daughter left to raise the others, could have told Rivke anything about her; she was the only one who had been old enough at the time of Zipporah's death to recall anything that might be told. But Etke was not a talker, not a teller of stories. In this way she was like Sol.

They were a strange family. Rivke had known the other remaining children, the middle children, Darda and Naman, only slightly. Not even slightly; really she hadn't known them at all, she had only *met* them (met them many times, it was true, but each time was like the first time: they were always polite to her, but also they were distant, and each time Rivke left them she discovered she couldn't remember anything either of them had said, which left her to wonder if they had stood silent while she did all the talking). They kept separate even from Sol, who never saw them either except at the large gatherings where Rivke met them again and again. Very strange people, she thought. She had ventured once to say this to Sol, though hesitantly; she knew how angry *she* became when a remark like this was made about one of her sisters or brothers, even about one of whom she had herself nothing very happy to say. But Sol said, indifferently, "In what way strange?" and Rivke found that she was at a loss to properly explain. They didn't seem to her *normal* somehow, she said; they were too hushed-up and small. Then she had to add that she didn't mean their height, that while they were indeed short, as Sol was short—evidently it was a family trait—it wasn't this that made them seem so small. They looked to her *diminished*, she said. "As if maybe they have shrunk." But this didn't satisfy her, and Sol in any case by this time appeared to have lost whatever interest he had had in the subject to begin with.

They were now, both Darda and Naman, long dead; they had died within months of each other—strange also. Darda had had a husband, Naman a wife, and the husband and wife had outlived the Vasilevskys to whom they'd been married (of this Rivke was sure because she recalled seeing both of them at both funerals) but she could not remember by how long. There were several children, too, as well as grandchildren; Rivke had never been able to keep straight which of them belonged to the brother, which to the sister. Oh, without a doubt the two had been unnaturally close. But it struck her now that this in itself was perhaps not so strange; that with Sol (but he was not then Sol, he was Sholom: his name before she knew him, before he came to America) a fatherless, motherless infant and Etke thus necessarily preoccupied with his care, the two middle children must have been left to look after themselves. Of course they would have attached themselves to each other. This would be natural. They had most likely raised one another.

So if they were strange, Rivke reflected, they had good reason to be so. How should they *not* be strange? Think of the terrible difference this would make in one's life—a childhood without parents. Such a loss would be engraved on the heart for a lifetime. And for Sol—Sholom, the baby? For him it had not even been a loss, but something worse than loss, something missing from the start.

She had in her mind now a picture of him, her husband, tiny child cared for by his sister who had also two other little ones to watch, those two who were full of resentment that the baby Sholom received so much attention. What could it have been like for him? A baby, then a small child, soon a young boy growing up with no one to look after him but his sister who was not more, really, than a child herself? This was a boy who had not within him a trace of memory of mother or father, who knew nothing of the demanding, worried type of love that only parent for child felt. And when he was grown? Grown, he was a man who lacked the memory of protection, of ordi-

nary safety, to which he was entitled—this unremarkable fact
of childhood to which anyone was entitled: the sense one had
(had and kept, long after it had lost meaning; carried in the
heart like the heart's own secret plan) of *run home where Mama
and Papa wait*. This he was without. This and much else also.
He knew only absence.

Rivke felt that she had to sit—she slammed shut the lid
of the toilet and sank down to it—so heavy was she with this
vision of him. Her husband! Her own! This orphan child with
no one in the world to care for him but the orphan sister so
miserly with words, a child deprived herself of everything necessary, deprived of everything but work—the impossible work
of raising, all by herself, this baby. This baby! Rivke thought,
her husband, Sol, Sholom. She was overwhelmed with pity
for him—it seemed to her she couldn't bear it. And now all
of a sudden she was in tears. This shocked her. Crying? Why
crying? The tears on her face felt like someone else's. She shook
herself—she grabbed her shoulders and pulled at them as if
she could shake away the person who was spilling tears on her.

But still came the tears. Came and came. She wept, she
thought, bewildered, as if her heart were breaking.

Then it was over; she had no idea how long it had gone
on. She felt tired—more than tired. She had the feeling that
everything inside her had been emptied out.

Her hands had settled loosely on her knees, palms up, as
if they were also tired. She couldn't think of what to do now.
After a minute she leaned over and tore off a long strip of toilet
paper; she dried her eyes and her cheeks and blew her nose.
And now? What now?

She thought she would stand up. There remained one
more room to be done—she reminded herself of this politely,
as if speaking to someone hired to do the work. *Yes? And so?*
Polite still. She waited. For a little while she wondered if perhaps she wasn't going to move after all. But then she did: she
stood, she took a moment to steady herself (she had a notion

that she might lose her balance, just standing still), and slowly she began to collect her things – broom, duster, rag, dustpan – and with them she left the bathroom.

In the kitchen – the worst job, the one she had purposely left for last – she went immediately to the stove. But it took only a few swipes with the dampened rag for her to see that she was wasting her time: the black grease was cooked right into the surface. She turned, next, to the sink, and here a glance was enough to tell her not to bother; it was so badly stained, whatever she did would make no difference. The cabinets, then – her mother's old battleground? The refrigerator?

Everything in the room seemed beyond cleaning – beyond, in any case, her ability to make clean. She had let things go for too long. Well, if so, she thought, it would be smarter to give up than to pretend she could do what she couldn't: if it couldn't be done, it couldn't be done. But as she stood thinking this over it occurred to her that there *was* one thing she could do, even now. Couldn't she still dust the blinds? Of course she could. If this was something small, at least it was something.

She began as high up the window as she could reach with the feather duster, slapping at the blinds and sending down on her head a shower of dust, which she then had to swat from her face. She worked with her eyes closed against the dustclouds, making her way downwards, the slats of the blinds rattling as she smacked them with the feathers – a good noise, she thought: she liked a job that gave off sounds of real work. Soon she came to the place halfway down the window where the blinds were stacked, and she had to open her eyes and lean over the television to get hold of the cord that released them. On the first tug of the cord they came down only a few inches; on the second, the right side slipped another inch or two but the left side didn't budge at all. She pushed the TV away a little from the window, toward the center of the table, to give herself more room, and she was reaching again for the cord –

ready to fight with it—when there in the left corner of the windowsill she spotted a shiny black box: a small, square box like one from a department store. A department store? It was so many years since she had been inside such a store, the box, she thought, must be very old. Or else it had once contained a present, something Myra or Rachel had bought. But it didn't look familiar to her. She picked it up, setting the feather duster on the table, and opened it. At the sight of the black crystal sparkling inside she cried out.

She stared at the beads, afraid to blink. How was it possible? Oh, it was *not* possible, she thought—it was not something real. How could it be real? And yet how could it not be real, how could she be imagining that here in her hand was a box containing the missing beads?

If she took her eyes off them for a second, would they disappear? Disappear *again*? The hand holding the box trembled. What was she supposed to do? She should do something—she couldn't think what. All over she was trembling now. Should she call Rachel? Yes, good, call Rachel. It was the only thing she could think of.

She kept the box in her hand as she went to the phone. She had to look for a long time at the list of numbers Scotch-taped to the wall—a list made by Rachel on a piece of shirt cardboard—before she was able to find the one she needed; and then after she found it she lost it again as soon as she took her index finger from it and began to reach for the receiver. Starting over at the top of the list, she read each name out loud, and when she came to Rachel's this time she read aloud the number too, and kept repeating it to herself, softly, like a chant, as she lifted the receiver. With painstaking care she picked it out on the dial.

Ringing. Her heart was beating too hard. She could feel it—her heartbeat—up where it shouldn't be: high inside her head.

Another ring. Now a click.

"Hello, this is Rachel Lieber. I'm not available right now, but if you wait until after the tone sounds and leave a message for me, I'll get back to you just as soon as I can."

Rivke shut her eyes. She was gripping the receiver so tightly her palm ached. "It's Grandma," she began—and then came the beep, and she remembered that Rachel had told her many times to wait for this sound to pass before she talked to the machine. She began again: "Rachel? It's Grandma. This is your grandma, Rachel, Grandma Rivke. I wanted only to tell you something. I wanted to tell you I have now the beads. This is what I called for."

She stopped; the silence at the other end unnerved her. Was this it? The message she had left seemed insufficient some-how. She tried to think—what else had she to say? "Rachel?" She cleared her throat. "You can still hear me? Listen. They're in a different box now, black not white this time. Still, I have them back. And they might think—the person who took them—that I wouldn't notice anything strange. But I ask you, what kind of person would think I'm so old I don't have any-more the brains to know that beads don't walk all by them-selves from one box into another, and from the bedroom to the kitchen? In the kitchen, Rucheleh! This is where I found them! By the window, right on the windowsill, in a corner hid-den for who knows how long by the little TV. You're sur-prised, I bet. I was also surprised." She stopped, embarrassed; she had forgotten for an instant that she was talking only to a machine. "That's all," she said. "I'm hanging up now. All right? This is your grandma, Rivke."

But she didn't hang up. She was still dissatisfied. She felt that she wasn't finished, although there wasn't anything more she had on her mind to say. It was talking to a machine, she thought: it was hard to feel that you had talked at all, when you didn't get an answer.

"Rachel?" She would try again, one more time. "Rachel, *still* can you hear me? Listen. Do you see how I was right? You see? I told you—didn't I tell you?—that this is what happens when you take in strangers to your house. You should remember, I told you this."

And now, finally, she hung up. She held the box close to her chest as she returned with it to the table.

Strangers, she thought. *That's right.* And she was supposed to trust such people! "My *wife*," they said. As if this were enough to convince you to trust. But why trust? Strangers, even if wives, husbands. And it could be any one of them—any one of them could have done this to her. Maybe it *was* Mark's wife. But maybe it wasn't. It could be somebody else too. Who could tell which one it was? They all brought in strangers to the house. All of them! With their magic words! "My wife," "my husband"! All but Rachel.

And why not Rachel? Because (oh, and what a pure shock it was to realize this!) despite her *own* efforts to convince the girl to do otherwise, Rachel remained, by choice, alone, unmarried. And why, Rivke asked herself, was she all the time arguing with her about this? When if she married it would be the same! More strangers! More magic words! What after all was so terrible about her being alone? It wasn't as if she was unhappy. That would be different. She wasn't unhappy. She didn't mind—she said she *liked* it. Think how hard it would be for her to find someone she liked as much as (or better than! It would have to be better than!) she liked being alone. Did such a person even exist? This "right man" Rachel talked about in such a joking tone of voice?

Oh, how she wanted at this moment to tell her, "Rachel, my darling, listen to me! There *is* no right man. A person like this does not exist."

It seemed urgent to tell her this, because evidently she didn't know—she thought it was a matter of time, of luck. *But think*, she wanted to tell her—*just think!*—*how your own mother felt so certain she had found for herself the "right man."* "Absolutely certain! Perfect for her! 'I love him, Mama, how I love him!' Like a broken record. You should have heard. I told her to think twice. Did she listen to me? No, because what did I know? 'He is the right one, believe me,' she said. And take a look what happened, look how it came out."

But Rachel, she knew, would not look at how it had come out. There was no point in saying this to her; when it came to her father, the child was impossibly stubborn. "What's so terrible?" Rivke imagined her saying. "She loved him then, she loves him now. What more do you want?"

What more? Even asked only by her imagination the question infuriated her. *Everything* more! Everything better! To think of how her daughter had fooled herself into believing that this husband was "meant for" her—oh, yes, this she had said also!—filled her with bitterness. No! Not meant for her! "For something better she was meant," Rivke would tell her granddaughter. "Yes? For what, then, tell me," Rachel would say to her. "For what?"

But Rivke didn't know for what. How could she answer this? And did it matter, when it was too late for an answer? When it was too late, even, to talk about it? Even if she had someone to talk *to* about it—for she could not talk to Rachel, not about this. Rachel would not speak of her father to Rivke; she refused. "This I won't discuss," she said—or she said nothing: she let her silence speak.

But once—just once—this came to Rivke suddenly, and she was chilled, remembering—she had spoken. More than spoken, she had screamed at her. They had, that time, come as close to arguing as they ever had. And it had started from nothing! They had been speaking quietly, in an ordinary way, of some small thing—some event in the past, in Rachel's childhood. There had been a recital or a school play, a dance festival, something of that nature. Rachel was recalling what she could of the day. She spoke of the dress Rivke had made her for this occasion; often she spoke of such details. Then she remarked that she had no recollection of her mother's pres-

ence at the event, and Rivke assured her that she was mistaken. "She loved you," Rivke told her, "naturally she was there."

"Well, it doesn't matter, does it?" said Rachel. "If she *was*
there, she might just as well not have been." And she said,
"Do you know, Grandma, I used to think of her sometimes
as a doll—a very precious one, not the kind you played with
but the kind people kept behind glass on a shelf in the dining
room, next to the good china. I had a friend whose mother
had a collection of those dolls: they were made of something
breakable and were dressed in the most beautiful costumes; we
weren't allowed to touch them. And somehow I made up a
story—you know how kids do—in which *she* was one, a life-
sized doll I was supposed to call Mommy. I told myself that
everyone knew she was really a doll—you and Daddy knew it
too—and we were all playing 'let's pretend.' I'd actually go for
days sometimes without touching her, because if I did, I thought,
I might break her and then I'd get in trouble."

"She was a delicate person," Rivke told her.

"Well, yes," Rachel said, "but that's not really what I mean.
It was more that . . . you know, when she *was* around, when
she wasn't tucked away in her room, she wasn't exactly in the
thick of things. She was just *there*. She didn't do much of anything; she didn't say much of anything—she was *like* a doll.
Whatever had to be done, you and Daddy took care of it. I
don't have a single memory of her ever managing anything on
her own, of her ever taking charge."

"Your father," Rivke agreed, "was very bossy."

And that was what did it: all at once Rachel was in a fury.
"Oh, Grandma, for God's sake! You are always *at* him! But
both of you did it. The two of you together. You treated her
as if she *was* a precious, stupid little doll."

"I?" Rivke said. She was astounded. When had Rachel ever
spoken to her this way?

"*Both* of you. Between the two of you, did she ever have
a chance to do anything? You didn't let her."

"I? What did I do?"

"Both of you! Both of you, dammit!"

Rivke could think of nothing to say that would calm her. And perhaps she should have remained quiet, then—but instead she spoke, she miscalculated. "Listen, *mamaleh*," she said—and she said it nicely, gently enough—"there are still a few things you don't know. You're young yet. When it comes to your father—"

A mistake. Rachel was now angrier. "Enough!" she said. "Enough—be still! I can't stand it! You keep tearing him down, but just *think*, Grandma—she *chose* him. For whatever reasons. I don't know why. I'm not *supposed* to know why, am I? Maybe she loved him be*cause* he didn't trust her with anything; maybe she didn't want to be trusted with anything—maybe she figured she was incompetent anyway. How should I know? You're the one who should know. You started it. Did you ever give her any credit for anything? Did you ever *let up* on her? Has it ever occurred to you that you might have intimidated her, scared her?"

"*I* scared her?" Shaken as she was, Rivke still managed to laugh. "Your father, the bully, used to yell at her—the windows would shake, he would yell so—and *I'm* the one who scared her? You don't remember how he used to yell?"

"I remember."

"So? So he made her sick."

"I don't think so," Rachel said. "I don't think that's what made her sick."

And Rivke understood, then, that it was necessary to back down. Her granddaughter was looking for a fight with her, and this was impossible—she would not do it. She would not fight, and she would not take seriously what had been said to her in anger: these things she would put out of her mind. "All right," she said. She spoke mildly. "It's possible of course that you know better. Who knows? Does anybody know what's the truth? No. Not me, not you. Isn't that so, Rucheleh?"

Maybe yes and maybe no. Rivke had no way of knowing how to interpret the silence that was Rachel's answer. But in any case they went on to speak of other things, and it was as if it had never happened—as if Rachel had never yelled at her, as if they had never come so close to something ugly.

In fact, Rivke could not help asking herself now if it *had* happened, if the conversation that was nearly a fight had indeed taken place or if perhaps she had dreamed it. Would Rachel really speak to her this way, say such things? Rachel who loved her so, who called her on the telephone every day? Who confided in her, trusted her? Why, the child thought of her as another mother! She was closer to her than she was to her mother. Was it to Myra she spoke of her work, of her future, of men? No—Rivke was sure not. "It's better not to talk to her"—this she had *told* Rivke. "She gets too upset. She can't get past, 'Oh, but you have no one to take care of you, you're all alone.' I tell her I *know* that, I like it that way. It drives her wild. She *cries*. Look, I know you're not crazy about it either, but at least you don't cry."

Cry? No, never. And never again would she complain. She would tell her: "No, you're right, it's better to take care of yourself, to do for yourself. Don't be fooled. You were right all along and I was wrong."

But she could guess how confused this would make her; she could hear her question, "What about Papa?" Because think after all how often the child had told her how lucky *she* had been. "If there was another around like Papa," she had said to Rivke many times, "it would be a different story. I'd get married tomorrow, I swear I would. But do you think you could find so good a man today?"

So good? The truth was it was hard for her to tell now just how "good" he had been. Everyone said this, everyone spoke of how fine a man Sol was—and not just family; once a fellow from the Workmen's Circle had told her that Sol was "the best man" he knew, that he was "a person on whom people feel they can always depend"—but for herself she didn't know anymore. She knew one thing, however. She knew that she needed him here with her—and he wasn't here.

And for this, even though she understood that it was not reasonable, she could not make herself forgive him. He was not here, and she needed him. She needed him much more now than she had when he was alive. *Now* was when she couldn't stand any longer her dirty kitchen and could do nothing about it; *now* was when she had to wash sheets and towels in the bathtub because she couldn't get to the laundromat— the laundromat which might just as well be halfway across the country as only across the street. And where was he? Where was he when she couldn't sleep? When she woke up terrified in the middle of the night? Where was he when strangers stole from her and then laughed at her while under her nose they slipped back what they had taken?

Where?

But now something peculiar happened. As she sat, her chair pressed against the radiator pipe, by the window which looked out onto the courtyard, the very window on the sill of which—she still could not believe it—her beads had been replaced, as she sat and tried to summon up a picture of him to scold, she found she couldn't. She couldn't imagine him at all.

How could she not imagine him? She closed her eyes and tried again: tried this time to picture him not as she usually did, but as he had been when they'd first met. But it was no better this way than the other. She couldn't *see* him—she could only remember what she had thought *about* him. *A nice-looking fellow, short, but well-dressed, very neat. Gentle. Good manners. A laugh that's pleasant to hear. . . .* This was what she remembered. Also that she had felt sorry for him, he was so lonely. He used to come around to the apartment on Essex Street, supposedly looking for her brother-in-law, but she knew better. From the beginning she knew better. He would come, Leah's husband wasn't home, and he would ask her to go for a walk with him. He was a nice boy, and an orphan; he wanted walks, so all right, she went for walks. They used to walk on the Williamsburg Bridge. Later on he gave her a bracelet—gold—and she kissed him. She felt that she had to kiss him: by then he had been taking her for walks, and sometimes to a show, for more than a year. But she didn't like to kiss—she had told him that already. She didn't like even to kiss her own family, and to kiss him (a stranger, still, even after a year of walks on the Williamsburg Bridge) didn't seem right to her. She was not a kissing person, she explained. But to him it was important: to hear him talk about it you would think it was a question of life and death. Also now he had bought for her this bracelet. So finally she kissed—he shouldn't be angry.

And then they were married. It looked to them to be the best thing to do. They would both be better off than they had been separately. Neither had been so happy, separately. And he loved her—this he told her many times as they walked together on the bridge. So that was that—they got married.

This was all that had happened. It was not such a great drama. It was an ordinary story—it was life, it was what happened to everyone. You start out you're all alone, young, not so happy. Maybe a little bit frightened, to be so alone in the world. Then comes someone and it's better to be together than to be alone. So you marry. You live with him, you grow old. And then one day he's gone and again you're alone. That was the whole story.

Except (she spoke to herself harshly now) that in the middle of this story there were seventy-two years. *Seventy-two years.* She and Sol had lived together for a longer time than some people *lived*, altogether. Their marriage *was* a life, it was what she had to show for life. What else did she have? Sol and her children—her life. So how then was it that she could not manage to conjure up an image of him—of the man who had made up a life with her, living beside her for almost three-quarters of a century? How?

And, again, she tried. She tried—she *concentrated*—and again came nothing: nothing more than a shadow, a vague, dark shape which even as she pictured it receded in her mind.

She was badly frightened now. What she wanted, suddenly, was to jump up—if she could jump!—and run—if she could run!—to the bedroom and look at the picture on her bureau, the picture of them in which she wore the black dress. She wanted to hold it in her hands. If she could hold it, look at it, she felt sure she would be reminded of everything. Not only of him. Also herself. Herself *then*, so long ago, in that dress. And *them*—the two of them, together. She felt if she looked at that picture she would *see*—she would see what they had been. Oh, she wanted more than anything to get up, to go and look at it! What stopped her—what had her frozen at the table, the little black box full of beads in her hand—was a fear so terrible she was paralyzed by it, a fear that was like certainty, like *truth*, it was so strong in her, that if she went to look, the picture would be gone—and that this time, *this* thing, would not be replaced, would never be returned to her, but would be gone for good, forever.

F
H   copy 1

Herman, Michelle

Missing

F
H   copy 1

Herman,   Michelle

AUTHOR Missing		
TITLE		
	10.00	

DATE DUE	BORROWER'S NAME	ROOM NUMBER
	Roz Lipton	